KT-522-747

Staffordshire Library and Information S

Please return or renew or by the last date sh

Beyond Redemption

As a child Jeff Dale witnessed the terrible aftermath of an atrocity. Elmer Drake killed three members of a family and when the surviving girl Cynthia went missing, Jeff vowed that one day he'd find her, no matter how long it took.

Ten years later, after finding a clue about Cynthia's fate, Jeff becomes a bounty hunter and follows the trail to the frontier town of Redemption. And in Redemption stalks a gunslinger who carries a gun in one hand and a cross in the other. A man with a rope-burn around his neck, called Elmer Drake. . . .

Beyond Redemption

I.J. Parnham

A Black Horse Western

ROBERT HALE · LONDON

ISBN 978-0-7090-9477-7

Robert Hale Limited
Clerkenwell House
Clerkenwell Green
London EC1R 0HT

www.halebooks.com

Typeset by
Derek Doyle & Associates, Shaw Heath
Printed and bound in Great Britain by
CPI Antony Rowe, Chippenham and Eastbourne

PROLOGUE

'Don't go in there, son,' Harold Dale said, his face ashen as he laid a hand on Jeff's shoulder. 'You're too young to cope with that.'

Jeff gave a dutiful nod, so his father turned away to talk to the other men. But he had left the door slightly open and, with the gap providing a tantalizing slice of the forbidden scene inside, Jeff rocked from side to side to see more.

Jeff was fourteen, and when Ben Ford and a delegation of men had arrived with news about trouble out at the Harris homestead he'd insisted he was old enough to ride off with his father.

His elder brother Samuel had taken the order to guard his mother and sister without complaint. His acceptance of his duty had annoyed Jeff, so he didn't want to return home without a tale to tell.

Sadly, it seemed he would have to do so when Ben pointed at tracks and then led the men away around the corner of the house. Forgotten about, Jeff shivered despite the warmth of the summer afternoon.

Then he peered at the gap in the door. It drew him forward.

His father hadn't looked as if he'd explain what was inside. Later, he would tell Samuel and then, later still, Samuel would tell him. That thought was enough to make Jeff disobey his father.

He checked that the men were involved with whatever they'd found beside the house. Then he scurried to the door and, being careful not to touch the wood and open the door wider, he put an eye to the gap.

At first he couldn't understand what he saw. Twilight appeared to bathe the room with a reddish hue. Then the thought hit him that the sun was high, so the light wasn't making the room red.

He dropped to his knees, knocking the door fully open. Then he stared straight ahead with his gaze locked on the three bodies lying on the floor, all of which looked like slaughtered livestock.

He didn't move until Ben's firm hand slapped down on his shoulder and gripped it tightly, making him flinch. With a gulp he looked at the hand. Then he turned his head back, but before he could face the horror again, he was lifted from the floor with his knees still bent.

He was swung away and deposited before his father, who considered him with concern narrowing his eyes.

'I'm sorry,' Jeff murmured. 'I had to look.'

'Maybe the next time I tell you not to do something, you'll obey me,' Harold said. 'Now, go home and tell your mother we're going after Elmer Drake. She's not to let anyone near the house she don't know.'

Last month Elmer had come looking for work. His father had chased him away while declaring he had no time for men like him. Unfortunately, the Harris family had lost their grown-up son and they needed help.

As the other men were moving for their horses, Jeff nodded. Then he rubbed his cheeks while opening his eyes wide to keep the tears at bay. He tried to avoid it, but he recalled what he'd seen inside, except he imagined it had happened in his own home to his own kin.

'If you hadn't sent him away, Father,' Jeff said with a shiver, 'he might have. . . .'

As Jeff fought back the tears, Harold asked the men who had already mounted up to wait. He knelt so that he could look up at his son.

'Try to forget what you saw, son, but remember this: most men are decent, but some men aren't. Learning to tell the difference can be the difference between living a happy life or . . . or what you saw in there.'

'I understand.' Jeff managed a smile, so Harold rose to his feet. 'But at least he didn't hurt Cynthia.'

Harold turned away, but then he swung back and stared at Jeff.

'You could be right,' he said. 'I don't reckon I saw their daughter in there.'

'I did a good thing, then?'

'You did a good thing. I'm proud of you.' Harold ushered him away and, when Jeff started walking with faltering paces, he hurried to the riders and raised his voice. 'Did anyone see Cynthia?'

Several men shrugged while others looked at the house with their expressions set sternly. Jeff could tell that few of them had looked inside and those who had, had been reluctant to check.

Ben took it upon himself to go inside. When he returned he confirmed Jeff's observation.

'Elmer killed Michael, Sallie and Clarence,' he said, 'but Cynthia's gone.'

'Elmer probably took her,' one man said with a heavy tone.

'Or she ran away,' Ben said.

'She's only fourteen,' Harold said. 'That could be as bad as Elmer taking her. But whatever the answer, we never stop searching until we find them both.'

A chorus of assent sounded as Ben and Harold mounted up. When Jeff got on his horse, several men cast him warm smiles that acknowledged his helpful role, and so he sat tall in the saddle.

The men rode past the house following the tracks Ben had found, while Harold drew aside to ensure that this time Jeff did as he'd been told. So after looking at the riders and quietly wishing he could join them, Jeff turned away and rode back towards home.

Fifty yards along the trail he glanced back. His

father was still watching him, so Jeff waved, making Harold Dale hurry after the other riders.

Jeff rode on for another fifty yards before he burst into tears. He hadn't stopped crying when he reached home.

CHAPTER 1

Ten years later. . . .

Something was wrong.

Jeff Dale peered down the slope at the campfire below, wondering what had given him that familiar feeling in his gut, a feeling that had saved his life on numerous occasions.

The three outlaws hadn't moved positions since he'd first found their camp an hour ago. Wilfred Jarrett was sitting with his back to him facing Cecil Cowper through the flames while listening to Cecil's animated tale, which involved plenty of gesturing.

Louis Keyes clearly hadn't thought this tale to be an interesting one, as he was lying on his back with his blanket pulled up over his face so that only his hat was visible.

As all three men were relaxed, Jeff could take them by surprise easily. Getting them to the law afterwards to claim the bounty on their heads would be harder, but Jeff hadn't lost a prisoner yet.

Then he identified his concern.

Louis had been asleep for an hour and yet he hadn't moved. Worse, when Jeff peered at his form in the flickering firelight, it didn't appear natural. It was almost as if blankets had been piled up to form the shape of a human.

Jeff winced. He moved away from the edge while turning and walked into the barrel of a gun, which had been aimed at his forehead. Behind the gun was Louis's grinning face.

'You won't be collecting no bounty on us,' Louis said before he raised his voice to shout, 'I've got him!'

As the men below whooped with delight Jeff raised his hands. Louis disarmed him, then ordered him to walk down the slope in front of him.

When he reached the fire, Cecil and Wilfred were standing together and smirking at their success.

'Enjoy yourself while you still can,' Jeff said, putting as much bravado into his tone as he could manage. 'Another dozen men are on your trail and they could be here at any moment.'

Wilfred stopped smiling and Cecil sneered.

'That's a lie,' Louis said. He stopped ten feet away with his gun aimed at Jeff's side. 'We haven't attracted that much interest.'

Unfortunately, Louis was right. His group's robbery spree had crossed two state lines, but their pickings had been meagre and so it'd taken time to build a reputation that had finally resulted in a $250 bounty being posted.

Jeff still shook his head in a confident way that made Wilfred scowl, confirming, Jeff hoped, that he had sown enough doubt for them to leave him alone.

'Make him tell us who's after us,' Wilfred said.

'I've got a better idea,' Louis said. 'If anyone is closing in on us, I reckon finding a shot-up body will make them turn back.'

Cecil gave an eager nod while Wilfred's mouth dropped open in horror. So, accepting that his only chance lay with the most reticent member of the group, Jeff looked at Wilfred.

'You face a few years in jail,' he said, keeping his tone level, 'but kill me and you'll all get the noose.'

Wilfred winced, then took a long pace towards Louis while shaking his head, forcing Louis to take a hurried backward step.

Jeff reckoned he'd be unlikely to get a better distraction than this. He broke into a run.

He'd covered two long paces and he was throwing up his arms ready to grab Louis when his target got his wits about him. Louis firmed his gun arm, but maybe his previous determination to shoot Jeff had been only bravado as he hesitated. That gave Jeff all the time he needed to reach him and bundle him over.

They tumbled to the ground and landed on their sides. Jeff slapped hands on his opponent's arms, ensuring he couldn't turn the gun on him.

12

For his part Louis squirmed and then, on finding that Jeff was holding him firmly, he braced his boots against the ground. He kicked off and rolled them both over until he'd pinned Jeff down.

On his back Jeff bucked Louis, and so the two men rolled back and forth, kicking up dust in their frantic efforts to gain the upper hand.

Footfalls sounded as Wilfred and Cecil moved forward to stand over them, where they waited for an opening. Jeff ignored them and concentrated on keeping the gun away from his body while Louis bent his arms as he strained to drag it closer.

After a momentary impasse while both men remained silent other than uttering the occasional grunt from their efforts, Louis's straining had an effect and he edged the gun closer to Jeff's face. His success made Wilfred and Cecil shout encouragement and, heartened, inch by inch, Louis moved the gun towards Jeff's forehead.

Jeff counteracted by digging in a heel and twisting them both on to their sides, seeking to trap Louis's gun arm between their bodies. Louis pushed back, but then he screeched and his gun arm went limp.

Jeff glanced down and saw that in an unfortunate turn of events Louis had knocked his elbow against a stone. Jeff took full advantage.

He released Louis's arm and wrested the gun from his weakened grip. Then he used his momentum to swing away from Louis, coming up on one knee facing the surprised Wilfred and Cecil.

13

Wilfred didn't react, but Cecil had already drawn his gun and he swung it towards Jeff. He had yet to get him in his sights when Jeff fired. His shot caught Cecil low in the chest making him double over. His gun fell from his slackening fingers and he dropped to his knees and then on to his side.

Jeff swung back to face Louis, who had shaken off his discomfort and was getting to his feet. His numbed arm dangled uselessly, but he still kicked off and leapt at Jeff.

With only a moment to react, Jeff fired, sending a slug into his opponent's upper chest at point-blank range. The shot didn't slow Louis's progress and he slammed into Jeff knocking him on to his back.

Trapped beneath Louis's body, Jeff struggled to free his gun hand, but when he shrugged the other arm free and raised Louis's head, blank eyes faced him. So, lying on his back, he looked at Wilfred who, in keeping with his previous reticence in confronting him, was busy surrendering.

'I didn't do nothing wrong,' he babbled as Jeff slipped out from under Louis and got to his feet. 'They made me do it. They gave me no choice. But I never did nothing.'

Jeff glanced at the still forms of Louis and Cecil and then offered his prisoner a smile.

'Save your excuses for the judge,' he said. 'But take my advice: get your story straight first. Then your babbling might be believed.'

Wisely, Wilfred didn't reply and, when he lowered

his head, Jeff sidestepped around the fire while keeping one eye on him until he reached the saddle-bags that he presumed contained their stolen goods.

He opened up the first bag. Numerous shiny objects were within.

'There's not much,' Wilfred said. 'We weren't worth a bounty.'

'The people you stole from think otherwise.' Jeff reckoned he'd already seen enough to warrant their notoriety, but he gestured at the other bags. 'Is this it all?'

'Yeah, except for the things we claimed for ourselves.'

Wilfred pointed at the bodies. Jeff searched through their pockets, finding mainly money. He faced Wilfred and raised an eyebrow.

With a rueful smile, Wilfred rummaged in his pockets and extracted bills along with a silver locket, which he moved to add to the pile of stolen items. But the locket caught the firelight and, in a shocking moment, it evoked a previously forgotten memory. Jeff reeled before he shook his head to get himself under control.

'The locket,' he said, his voice gruff as he held out a hand.

With a bemused expression on his face, Wilfred did as he'd been asked. When the locket sat on his palm, Jeff examined it.

The locket was oval, an inch long on its longest side, and smooth, as it should be. He flicked it open.

It was empty, although the clasp on the back could have once held a lock of fair hair.

'There was nothing in it when I found it,' Wilfred said, his voice also gruff as he picked up on Jeff's mood.

'After all these years I didn't expect there would be,' Jeff murmured, speaking to himself more than to Wilfred.

'Are you saying you know who owned it?'

Another memory that he hadn't recalled for many years came back to Jeff. He turned the inside of the locket to the firelight. On the back were what at first sight appeared to be scratches. Except that Jeff knew that he had made them with a pin when, ten years ago and just before Elmer Drake had ridden into town, he had marked out the initials 'C' and 'J'.

Jeff clasped the locket in his hand and advanced a long pace.

'Where did you get this?' he demanded.

Wilfred gestured over his shoulder vaguely.

'I found it in a wagon a day's ride out of Redemption close to this trading post. . . .' Wilfred's voice trailed off. Then he stood tall and, as a small smile played on his lips, he appeared to gather his composure for the first time. 'If you want, I can take you there.'

Jeff looked aloft, sighing. Then, in acceptance of the deal that was clearly on Wilfred's mind, he returned the smile.

16

'Do that,' he said, 'and you might just become the only man who's ever got away from me.'

CHAPTER 2

'How much?' Norton Hope asked when John Stuart sat down.

John glanced around the trading post to confirm that, aside from Norton's companions Albert Shaw and Oscar Lewis, the post was empty. Even the owner, Roy Metz, had got bored with watching them stretch out their funds by drinking slowly and he had slipped away into another room.

'I searched Redemption until I found someone who'd give me the best deal,' John said. 'Then I had to haggle to—'

'How much?' Norton said while Albert and Oscar echoed his plea.

John gulped, hinting that despite his reassuring information, good news wouldn't be forthcoming.

'I got us . . . two hundred and sixty dollars.'

John smiled even though this was lower than even the lowest amount they had feared they'd get.

'That was for all the gold?' Albert asked after an

uncomfortable silence had dragged on.

'Yes,' John said defensively. 'We hadn't collected much and the price has dropped.'

'Three months,' Oscar spluttered, finding his voice at last. 'And all we got is two hundred and sixty dollars between four men.'

'It's worse,' Albert said. 'We put in a hundred dollars to buy the equipment and supplies. That means all that hardship we suffered got us forty dollars each.'

While Albert and Oscar cast dark glances at each other about this unwelcome conclusion to their gold prospecting operation, John and Norton headed to the bar.

'Don't be annoyed with us,' Norton said. 'We knew it'd be bad, but until you returned we could still hope it'd turn out well.'

John nodded. 'I've had longer to get used to the disappointment. Now I reckon we came out of this with more money than when we started and that means we have enough to buy new supplies and try again somewhere else.'

Norton considered whether he wanted to try again. Three months ago it had felt different when they'd fetched up in Monotony at the end of another gruelling cattle drive. They had all vowed never to join another drive.

While they had money in their pockets, buying them time to consider what they should do next, John had sold them the idea of searching for gold in the Redemption Mountains.

Anything that didn't involve mobile beef had sounded good to the others. And, as it turned out, for the first month they'd enjoyed themselves with nightly liquor, with campfire stories and every day starting with the feeling that today they'd make their fortune.

Then the liquor ran out and the stories dried up, so their failure to find anything other than the occasional small nugget had worn down their enthusiasm. Despite the setbacks, John had remained optimistic and, when he considered the alternatives, Norton found to his surprise that he was too.

'Perhaps we should try again,' he said, 'and after he's grumbled for a while I reckon Oscar will come with us. But Albert really has had enough.'

'Don't worry. He'll come round to our way of thinking, like he did the last time.'

John winked and then returned to the table where Albert proved that Norton had been right. For the next ten minutes he grumbled about how he hated gold more than he hated beef. When he'd finished his drink, he stood up.

'This is where we part company,' he said, his comment making the others gasp even though they had been expecting it. 'I'll head into Redemption and see what work I can find.'

'We've worked together for three years,' John said, his matter-of-fact tone showing he'd considered what to say beforehand. 'We've stood by each other and survived many a scrape. You're disappointed, but you won't find nothing better in Redemption.'

While Oscar and Norton murmured their support of John's well-chosen words, Albert frowned.

'I have to go,' he said with determination. 'I can't face another three months out there.'

He nodded to each man in turn and, acknowledging that this was hard to deal with, the rest stayed seated and silent until Norton got up and shook Albert's hand while murmuring a goodbye.

Oscar followed his lead, but John counted out forty dollars from their profits and added Albert's twenty-five dollar stake. He handed it all to him without comment.

Then Albert headed to the door. Norton and Oscar watched him go while John counted the rest of their money. When he looked up, Norton and Oscar were glaring at him.

'You should have said goodbye,' Oscar said.

'I didn't need to.' John tucked the money in his pocket. 'He'll be back.'

Oscar shook his head, but John's determination to find a bright outlook in any situation made Norton smile and he started making a list of their requirements for their new expedition. He'd detailed only ten dollars' worth of supplies when the door crashed open and Albert hurried back in.

'I knew you'd be back,' Oscar said, eliciting an amused snort from John, but Albert only gulped and then pointed at the door.

'You were followed,' he said, his voice high-pitched with worry. 'And they look like trouble.'

They had sent John into Redemption alone because they'd heard tales of prospectors being waylaid and they'd thought that four men would attract undue attention. Albert had reckoned that John going alone was riskier. So, while he told them he'd known this would happen, they made for the door.

Four riders had arrived. They had spread out facing the trading post, which they were considering with eager eyes and wide grins.

'They probably just want supplies too,' Norton said as Albert closed the door. He wrapped an arm around Albert's shoulders when he disagreed and ushered him away from the door. 'Maybe if you're that edgy, you should stay with us.'

This comment made John and Oscar laugh, so when the four newcomers entered their spirits had been restored slightly. The four who had ridden in leaned back against the counter and watched John and his partners work their way around the room, noting what they needed and, apart from Albert, avoiding looking at the newcomers. Then, after a few minutes, Roy came in from the back room.

He noted the new arrivals and scurried from view. That sight made Norton walk across the post to stand before the four strangers.

'You men looking for anything?' he asked,

keeping his tone pleasant.

His question made his friends stop considering the stock in order to hear the response. A burly man stepped forward.

'Only you,' he said. The sour liquor on his breath made Norton's eyes water.

'What can—?'

Norton didn't complete his question as the man launched a scything backhanded punch at his face. At the last moment Norton jerked away from the upward blow, but it still caught him a stinging slap to the cheek that made him spin round before he dropped to his knees.

He shook his head, seeking to regain his senses, but it had the opposite effect, making him dizzy, and he keeled over on to his side. He slapped both hands to the floor and sought to raise himself, but his limbs shook and then gave way, depositing him back on the floor.

A swinging kick crunched into his ribs, rolling him on to his back. He lay there watching the ceiling swirl while he struggled to focus his vision. His attackers appeared to consider him dealt with, as they then turned their attention on to the others.

Thuds and blows sounded, interspersed with orders given by a man, who identified himself as Dewey Shark. Then cries of pain rent the air, and those cries were all made by Shark's friends.

A crash sounded as the table around which Norton and his partner had been sitting collapsed.

Then a heavy weight slammed into Norton's right shoulder, rolling him on to his side.

He thought he'd been kicked and he moved away from the expected next blow, but then he found that Albert had been thrown against him. The jarring knock at least helped him to focus his eyes and, hoping that his strength had returned, he again put a hand to the floor.

This time his arm didn't shake and he levered himself up to a sitting position. After a worrying moment when his vision darkened, he focused on the scene before him. It made him wish he'd slipped into unconsciousness instead.

Albert was lying on his chest groaning while Oscar lay draped over the counter with his arms dangling. A man whom Norton had overheard being addressed as Drago was raising his head to consider his bruised and bloodied face. He took but a moment to decide he was out cold.

Only John had remained standing, but that was only because he was being held up by Lester and Gene, two of the newcomers, while the leader of their group, Dewey, strutted in front of him. Held aloft was the $260 they'd worked for so long to gather.

'Where's the rest?' Dewey demanded.

The sight of the money in someone else's hand made anger rage in Norton's guts. He got to his feet and stood hunched over with his legs planted wide apart. His movement made the other men look at him, but they dismissed him as a threat with sneers before they turned their attention back to John.

'You've got it all,' John murmured.

'You were gone three months. There's more.'

When John shook his head, Dewey gestured and Drago moved in to deliver a swinging blow to his stomach that made him fold over. Then Drago grabbed his hair to raise his head and thundered a fierce uppercut to his chin that stood him up straight.

John tried to wrest himself free, but Lester and Gene had tight grips. Drago rolled his shoulders and swung back a fist, but then he stilled his motion when he saw Norton coming towards him, his stumbling gait making heavy footfalls that echoed around the post.

'We've got no more,' Norton muttered. 'Leave or we throw you out.'

Drago advanced on him. Norton hurled a weak punch that only parted air a foot short of its target. The effort swung him round and he was too weak to resist when Drago grabbed his shoulders and held him securely.

'Wrong,' Drago muttered in his ear. 'You're the one who's leaving.'

Then he pushed him towards the door. Norton staggered on for three paces before he lost his footing. He went tumbling, rolling twice before he fetched up against the closed door, making it rattle.

He tried to get to his feet, but a wave of dizziness

hit him. When the nausea receded, he found he was sitting on the floor with his back to the wall.

Drago was looming over him. When he saw that Norton had regained his senses, he grabbed his vest front and regarded him with a raised eyebrow and a silent question.

'You can hit me all day,' Norton murmured while dragging in gasps of air, 'but we still won't have any more money.'

'Obliged for the offer.'

Drago bunched a fist and moved to punch him in the face making Norton jerk his head away, but the blow didn't come. Instead, the door crashed open. A screech sounded and a heavy thud shook the wall.

Norton turned back to see Drago's feet dangling and twitching. Bemused, he looked up and saw that another newcomer had arrived. A tall man was towering above him, so that Norton couldn't see his face. He was holding Drago off the floor by the throat.

The man hurled his victim away and Drago smashed into the counter head first with a sickening crack of timber and bone. Then the newcomer paced across the post, his long coat rustling in the breeze from the open doorway, to face up to the other men.

The three men stared at him with shocked eyes that were open so wide they could be facing an apparition. Dewey got over his shock first and confronted him, but the newcomer batted him aside with a backhanded swipe that made Dewey go reeling across the post towards Norton.

The stricken man fought to bring his progress to a halt before he reached the door, but Norton intervened by raising a leg. Dewey tripped over it and fell all his length as he slid out through the doorway.

The two men who remained standing released John to take on their adversary together and although John couldn't have helped him, the newcomer didn't need any help. He punched Lester in the chest with a pile-driver of a blow that made him drop, a silent scream of pain on his lips that he appeared unable to voice.

Even before his knees had hit the floor, the unstoppable man had grabbed Gene. With no discernible effort he lifted him high off the floor where he held him by the throat while watching him with his head cocked to one side.

Gene's strangulated bleats became weaker and his twitching became ever more frantic until with one last shake he stilled. The man let him drop and turned his attention to the kneeling Lester, who stared at his colleague with a mixture of shock and pain.

Then, while rubbing his chest, he sought to get up, but before he could gain his feet his assailant grabbed the back of his jacket and held him bent double. Then he ran him at the counter and smashed his forehead against the rim.

Another sickening crack sounded and Lester joined his colleagues lying in broken heaps on the floor. Norton heard scrambling in the doorway and Dewey's worried face appeared before the group's leader took the sensible course of hurrying away.

The tall man didn't register that he'd fled and, almost as if this was the way he usually entered an establishment, he calmly stepped over the bodies at the counter and slapped a fist on the wood.

'Service,' he said using a quiet tone.

Oscar and Albert were still lying unconscious, so John came over to Norton and helped him to his feet. They looked at each other with bemused expressions, but neither man spoke until they joined their saviour at the counter.

'We're obliged,' John said cautiously, 'that you arrived when you did.'

The man looked at John, making him flinch; then, when he turned his gaze on to Norton, Norton could tell what had troubled his friend. The man's eyes were darker than any eyes he'd ever seen before so that they seemed to bore into his very soul.

'Those men will burn in hell,' the man said.

His intense gaze troubled Norton and he moved away. With repeated slaps to their cheeks, he encouraged Oscar and Albert back to consciousness. When both men stirred, John resumed his questioning.

'Who are you?' he asked.

The man leaned back against the counter.

'Elmer Drake,' he said.

CHAPTER 3

When Jeff Dale first saw the blue ribbon of the river, Wilfred Jarrett bade him to halt. Wilfred then pointed downriver and across the plains, indicating the distant and unseen town of Redemption.

'The wagon came from over there,' he said, before he pointed upriver. 'I sneaked into it past that long bend and took the locket. You should be able to pick up the wagon's tracks and follow it.'

'Provided the owner is still alive,' Jeff said.

'I stole, but I never harmed nobody,' Wilfred said without conviction. Then he shrugged. 'You going to tell me about the woman who owned the locket?'

'Nope,' Jeff snapped.

He beckoned Wilfred to follow him and without comment the man did as he was ordered. So far he had been as good as his word. He'd answered Jeff's questions and had brought him here without prevarication. He hadn't tried to escape and he had

29

appeared willing to keep his side of a bargain that Jeff had never thought he'd make.

For the last five years Jeff had earned a living as a bounty hunter. He had always found his quarries, the unsatisfactory conclusion to the childhood incident that had led to his current search having motivated his single-minded devotion. Ever since he had captured Wilfred the unknown fate of the locket's owner had never been far from his thoughts.

Ten years ago, an itinerant worker, Elmer Drake, had destroyed the Harris family in Dirtwood. Both parents and the son had been killed. The daughter Cynthia had gone missing, never to be found.

The search for her and for Elmer had occupied everyone's thoughts that summer and many people had travelled far without success, but then harvest time followed by a harsh winter had turned everyone's attention away from the troubling matter.

The following spring the settlement elders decided with regret that they could do nothing now. Elmer would receive justice only if others found him, while Cynthia must be dead. In fact, she had probably died before the search had started.

For the next two years occasional messages arrived about possible sightings of Elmer and once of Cynthia, but they were always vague and unsatisfying. Then even those snippets dried up and, although life returned to normal, the community never trusted strangers again.

Later, his elder brother Samuel being groomed to

take over the family homestead, Jeff had left home to seek his own way. In Prudence he worked in a stable where his desire to see justice done had encouraged him to join a posse after the ostler had been robbed.

Then, when he was the one who had found the outlaw, he accepted an offer to be a deputy sheriff. But before long the poor wages and the challenging Wanted posters on the law office wall encouraged him to seek a greater financial reward for his skill in finding outlaws.

He'd been successful, but he had often thought about the man who had neither received justice nor attracted a bounty. To Jeff the lack of a financial incentive didn't matter, as he would gladly bring Elmer Drake to justice for nothing, no matter what he had to do to find him.

That thought made him wonder whether he should confide in Wilfred and so hear another viewpoint. So when they found a sheltered spot near the river to settle down for the night, Jeff spoke to him using a softer tone than hitherto, picking up on their conversation of an hour ago.

'Cynthia Harris was a young woman,' he said.

'A sweetheart?' Wilfred asked.

'We were fourteen and if . . . if she'd lived, we could have been.' Jeff smiled, recalling one of his few good memories of her. 'I scratched our initials into the locket, but my brother caught me and we fought over her. He won, but he didn't get to scratch his initial.'

His light tone made Wilfred laugh.

'Why has a dead girl's locket surfaced after all these years?' he wondered.

Jeff frowned, but having overcome his reticence to speak, as they made camp he told Wilfred about the incident in Dirtwood.

'So,' he said finishing off, 'she could be alive.'

Wilfred looked aloft, appearing to cast his mind back.

'It was dark when we happened across the wagon,' he said, 'and I didn't see nobody, but I saw a woman's clothing.'

'No answer other than that she's alive will cheer me, but finding out the truth is sure to be better than the fate that's stuck in my mind.'

Then, with Wilfred offering no additional insights, in a relaxed frame of mind Jeff retired for the night. For the first time since capturing Wilfred, he slept soundly.

Strangely, when he awoke, he wasn't surprised that Wilfred hadn't taken advantage of his relaxed state. So, when they set off riding upriver, he kept only half of his attention on his prisoner.

As they closed on the spot Wilfred had indicated the previous night, Jeff resolved that after he'd confirmed Wilfred's story and used up his useful knowledge, he would honour his side of the bargain and release him. Later, when he found the wagon owner, he would hand back the locket and report that two of the robbers were dead while the third had escaped.

32

Thirty minutes later that resolution died.

He had expected that at best he would find only evidence that the wagon had been by the river, but as it turned out the owner was still there, or at least a body was. Jeff let Wilfred approach the scene first. Even his horrified scowl didn't convince Jeff of his innocence.

The burnt-out remains of the covered wagon lay on its side while bones lay scattered, animals and buzzards having removed evidence of the nature of the death that had been meted out here. Wilfred stayed on his horse as he moved around the wagon and then returned to Jeff, where he faced an aimed six-shooter for the first time since their first meeting.

'Her body?' Jeff asked.

'It's hard to tell.' Wilfred considered the gun. 'Except she was alive the last time I saw her.'

Jeff scowled. 'You claimed you never saw her.'

'I didn't mean it that way. I meant I heard her snoring.' When Jeff maintained his grim visage Wilfred sighed. 'I wouldn't have brought you here if I knew we'd find this, would I?'

Jeff had to admit that this was a valid point, but the tragic end to his search made him shake his head.

'I don't know how you think,' he said as he dismounted.

He kept one eye on Wilfred while he examined the scene. Sadly, nothing substantial had survived the fire, so there were no hints about the owner's identity and certainly nothing that would tell him why she had the locket.

He found a gnawed skull and placed it on a small mound. It was smaller than others he'd seen and he judged it to be female. He hunkered down and stared into the blank eyeholes wondering if he'd found the last resting place of a woman he'd assumed had died ten years ago.

The unresolved nature of this end to his quest gave him no comfort. In a sombre frame of mind he scraped out a hole with a singed plank and laid the bones inside. He covered the hole and took one last look at the scene to preserve the memory. Then he mounted up.

Wilfred hadn't offered to help with the burial. When Jeff signified that they should head north to Redemption, seeking to go back along the river and trace the route the dead woman had taken to get here, Wilfred didn't move.

'I've completed my side of our bargain,' Wilfred said. 'It's time for you to complete yours.'

'Our deal's off,' Jeff said. 'I'm handing you over to the law in Redemption.'

Wilfred narrowed his eyes, although this minor reaction showed he hadn't expected any other response.

'I stole from her. I didn't kill her.'

His tone sounded honest, but Jeff still gestured for him to ride on. When Wilfred didn't move, Jeff hunched forward in the saddle.

'Perhaps you didn't, but maybe your friends

returned and killed her.' Jeff watched Wilfred wince, accepting that this could have happened. 'But either way, the law can decide the truth while I find out what I can about her; something that you can't help me with.'

Wilfred opened his mouth, his red face showing he was minded to provide an oath-laden retort, but then he flinched, his eyes glazing as he clearly detected the offer hidden within the threat.

Wilfred moved on. He rode with hunched shoulders for a mile with Jeff following. Then he sat up straight and waited for Jeff to join him. His pensive expression promised that he'd thought up a new version of events that wouldn't run counter to what he'd claimed earlier.

'The wagon,' he said, 'picked up supplies from a trading post outside Redemption. We followed it here. We didn't get close enough to see the owner properly, but she couldn't have been Cynthia. She was a middle-aged woman. We thought she was a prospector heading to the Redemption Mountains on a damn fool mission to look for gold.'

'Obliged,' Jeff said with a sigh of relief. 'But that won't stop me handing you over to a lawman.'

'Hey,' Wilfred spluttered. 'That's—'

'That's not enough.' Jeff winked. 'On the other hand, you've got the rest of the day to come up with something better.'

Wilfred glared at him, but then with a snap of the reins he moved on. Jeff followed while smiling at his predicament.

As it turned out, as they rode on beside the river Wilfred didn't offer anything more. Jeff wondered if he had, in the end, told him the truth, but having heard several versions of the robbery, he was no longer interested in Wilfred's fate.

Sundown was an hour away when they reached the trading post. Jeff dismounted and then gestured for Wilfred to accompany him inside.

'Do you remember a prospector heading south for the mountains a week ago?' he asked the owner, Roy.

'Plenty of prospectors pass through,' Roy said with practised disinterest. 'Don't remember none of them.'

'That's unfortunate.' Jeff fished in his pocket for money and the sight of an eagle made Roy rub his jaw.

'Can tell you a tale about what happened here three days ago.' Roy's fingers inched across the counter. 'Four prospectors were ambushed by some no-good men from Redemption. Then the varmints got what they deserved when this man saved—'

'Not interested in them.'

Jeff drew the coin away from Roy's grasping fingers. He glanced at Wilfred and, with a raised eyebrow, he silently told him this was his last chance to be useful and so avoid a trip to Redemption.

'We're only interested in Maggie Cartwright,' Wilfred said while avoiding catching Jeff's eye after confirming he knew more than he had divulged previously. Clearly he knew that this woman was the owner of the burnt-out wagon in which he had found Cynthia's locket. 'She'd been sick and she was coughing.'

'That's the interesting thing,' Roy said, eyeing the silver coin with an eager smile. 'The man who saved the prospectors had been in here before and that visit was shortly after Maggie left.'

Wilfred frowned while Jeff considered this story, wondering whther it helped him.

'Was there a young woman,' Jeff said, after deciding that it probably didn't, 'with any of these people?'

'No.'

'Does the name Cynthia Harris mean anything to you?'

Roy cast a forlorn look at the coin as he struggled to find an answer that'd please his customer.

'I don't know about no young woman, but I do know about that man. He was tall and strong, and the thing I'll never forget is his eyes. They were as dark as night and they could turn your soul to ice.'

Wilfred cast Jeff an amused glance, but Jeff ignored him. Coldness was creeping across his chest, making him shiver. Then a memory he hadn't recalled for a long time came back to him.

Ten years ago, a tall man had stood in the doorway to his parents' house. His father barred his way while explaining he didn't have any work. So the man glared over his shoulder at Jeff, and his eyes had been dark.

Afterwards the man had started working for the Harris family.

Jeff had hoped the locket would help him find Cynthia and that that would lead him to Elmer Drake, but he hadn't considered that it might get him close to Elmer straight away. Now the thought made him sway and he had to grab the counter to stay upright.

'Obliged,' he said. He shoved the dollar across the counter and make for the door.

As he left Wilfred resumed questioning Roy. Outside, Jeff waited impassively, his head buzzing with the possibilities that this version of events had opened up.

When Wilfred emerged he wisely took heed of Jeff's mood and didn't complain when they set off to Redemption.

'He didn't know much else,' Wilfred said after a while. 'But he knew the man's name.'

Jeff took a deep breath. 'Elmer Drake?'

'Sure,' Wilfred said. 'That enough to keep me out of jail?'

'No.' Jeff offered a grim smile. 'But then again, if Elmer's around, that'll be safest place to be.'

CHAPTER 4

The setting sun was at his back when Jeff rode into the bustling town of Redemption.

It had been twenty years since a gold rush had fuelled a boom town that had lived, thrived and died all within a year. Then, long after most people had accepted that there was no more gold to be dug up, silver had been found at Bleak Point.

Now a railroad was being built to come up from Monotony past Redemption and across the Barren Plains to the silver mine. All the accompanying industry in the area had provided a more stable reason for people to settle and for businesses to grow, and so the small town had spread.

Now solid, prosperous-looking buildings were on both sides of a long main drag, and it took Jeff a while to find the law office, close to the station. Wilfred was no help, remaining as silent as he had been since leaving the trading post. But, despite his surly attitude, he hadn't confronted Jeff and nor had he tried to ride off.

'You're wrong about me,' Wilfred said when Jeff signified that he should dismount.

'I hope so,' Jeff said. He picked up the largest saddle-bag and draped it over one shoulder before dismounting.

Wilfred dismounted too and, in a show of defiance, he stood before Jeff with his hands on his hips.

'Keep me out of jail,' he said, raising his chin as he made an offer that Jeff had been expecting for the last hour, 'and I'll tell you where Elmer Drake is.'

Jeff walked up to him, failing to suppress a smile on hearing Wilfred's obviously hollow promise. Then Jeff turned him round and pushed him on towards the law office. Wilfred was looking back over his shoulder at him as both men went inside.

'Got several hundred dollars' worth of stolen goods outside,' Jeff said to Eddie Bell, the deputy town marshal who was sitting behind his desk.

'Marshal Root will want to hear about it,' Bell said, 'just as soon as he's dealt with her.'

Bell nodded to the corner of the office where, to Jeff's amusement, he saw that the exasperated marshal was being berated by an old and loud nun.

'Sister Angelica,' Root said, using a sharp tone that showed he'd been trying and failing for a while to interrupt her flow of complaints, 'I've said that I'll do what I can.'

'What *you* can do,' Angelica said with disdain, 'is never good enough. My work was hard enough

40

before one of my helpers went missing. Unless you find him immediately, sick people will suffer.'

While Jeff waited for the outcome of this debate, he dropped the saddle-bag on the floor and stood over it.

'I wasn't lying,' Wilfred urged when the deputy turned his attention back to the argument. 'I know.'

'And only now when jail beckons do you tell me that.'

'I've only just figured it out.' Wilfred glared at him and then, having made his offer, he joined the deputy in watching the marshal and the nun gesticulate at each other.

If Wilfred had claimed to have information, Jeff would have ignored him. Every man he'd brought in had claimed to have information on something, and it had never worked. But this time Wilfred was claiming he was piecing together the situation in the same way that Jeff was.

While he struggled to decide, Root raised his voice in an attempt to end the meeting.

'Redemption's townsfolk are grateful,' he said, 'that the sisters of the Sacred Cross care for the sick and injured, but—'

'But,' Angelica said, 'you won't find out where Mark's gone.'

'If this Mark worked for you for six months, he's probably just had enough of . . .' Root trailed off from concluding his insult when Angelica favoured him with a withering look.

41

'I'll see you every day until you find him,' she declared. Then, without waiting for a response, she turned on her heel and strode off. She stopped to consider Jeff. 'What are you smirking about?'

'I like a woman with spirit,' Jeff said with a wide smile that died quickly when Angelica stared straight through him.

'I'm not a woman. I'm a sister of the Sacred Cross.'

Jeff decided that any response would be unlikely to be received well so he said nothing, leaving her to glare at Wilfred. When he wisely avoided her eye, she strode on to the door.

'What's your story?' Marshal Root asked with a weary sigh when the door had been slammed shut.

'I thought it a good one,' Jeff said. 'But it's not as interesting as that one sounded.'

Root shrugged. 'Apparently some poor worker who'd been helping out at her hospital has gone missing. Can't blame him.'

'It sounds as if people going missing happens often around here.'

Root narrowed his eyes, clearly affronted by the implication that he wasn't in control.

'It does, but this is different. Now, how are you going to waste my time?'

Jeff took a last glance at Wilfred, then gestured at the saddle-bag at his feet.

'I chased three outlaws for the bounty. They attacked me and I killed two of the varmints.' He removed the folded up Wanted poster that provided the details from the saddle-bag. 'The third one high-tailed it away. I never saw him again.'

Ten minutes later he and Wilfred were leaning on the bar in the nearest saloon.

'Obliged you accepted my offer,' Wilfred said.

'I didn't say I had,' Jeff said. 'I just figured that if your guess don't amount to anything, I can still hand you over to the law.'

'I thought as much,' Wilfred grumbled before he ordered whiskeys. When they arrived, he didn't speak for a while as he considered his drink. When he did his speech was slow and deliberate. 'I reckon the answer lies in what the trading post owner said.'

Jeff shrugged. 'I'd worked that out. Elmer helped those prospectors, so they probably know where he went, except they'll be heading back to the mountains. You got more than that?'

'I heard the rest of Roy's tale.' Wilfred waited until Jeff grunted with encouragement. 'Three raiders died from their injuries; one returned here. I figure we should find him and ask him what he knows about Elmer.'

Jeff considered this guess, nodding until he reached a conclusion.

'That's some mighty fine figuring.' He slapped Wilfred's back and downed his whiskey in a single gulp. 'If we get a decent answer, it'll keep you out of a jail cell.'

Then, with the smiling Wilfred leading, they went in search of the survivor. As it turned out, even though Jeff still didn't trust Wilfred, he found their quarry more readily than Jeff would have done.

Jeff's method was quietly to find people who would talk, paying them for every scrap of information, then later sifting out the truth. Wilfred's method was the more direct one of asking around with casual interest and, probably because he looked too downbeat to be trouble, he got answers.

An hour after leaving the law office, Jeff and Wilfred were sitting at a table in a dingy saloon sharing a whiskey bottle with an inebriated and sullen Dewey Shark.

'I'm not talking about Elmer Drake,' Dewey said with a wide-eyed glare of shock in reply to Wilfred's cautious opening question. 'When dead men walk, I stay in the saloon.'

Dewey slapped a hand on Wilfred's arm and gripped it, making Wilfred flash Jeff a glance that asked him to take over the questioning.

'I aim to find him,' Jeff said and, when Dewey didn't reply, he made his usual offer. 'I'll pay you to tell me where he went.'

Dewey shivered, then reached for the whiskey bottle. His hand shook as he refilled his glass.

'He went to hell, except he came back.'

'And then where did he go?'

Dewey fingered his collar while mumbling to himself, presumably because Jeff wasn't responding in the way he expected. Then he gestured, indicating a southward direction.

'He joined those prospectors and I know where they've gone, but you haven't got enough money to make me go with you.' He raised his hand and watched it until the tremor subsided. 'Elmer Drake died. I saw him breathe his last with my own eyes. But then he rose up again and his trip to hell had given him the strength of ten men. He tore us apart like we were kids' dolls.'

Dewey grabbed his glass and knocked back his drink, spilling most of it down his vest front in his haste.

'I've got enough money to let you drink yourself to death,' Jeff said. 'Take me far enough to pick up Elmer's trail. Then leave. You don't need to see him ever again.'

Dewey stared at him with tortured eyes, but after a few moments the offer made him lick his lips. He gave a barely perceptible nod.

'You can't ever stop me seeing him,' he murmured. 'If I don't drink myself into a stupor, I see the dead walking again every night when I close my eyes.'

With a sigh he closed his eyes and his head flopped down to lie on the table. In moments rasping snores sounded and Jeff reckoned that despite the man's anguish of the last few minutes, they were contented ones.

'How is the newest member of our group feeling today?' Norton Hope asked, sitting beside Elmer Drake.

Elmer appeared lost in thought, as he had been since he'd joined them three days ago, but he tore his gaze away from watching the other men light the night's fire and turned to consider him.

'Elmer's planning,' he said.

His low tone and his dark, hooded eyes suggested that he didn't want to chat. He'd kept his own company and he had spoken only rarely since the incident at the trading post, but nobody had minded.

The fight had shown them what he was capable of, and everyone had felt safer when he'd agreed to join them on their latest expedition. Even Albert hadn't wavered before he'd agreed to stay with them.

Strangely, when Norton had thought back to the discussion in the post about what they should do next, he couldn't remember anyone actually asking Elmer to join them. He had just done it.

'Does that mean,' Norton said, 'you have an idea about where to find gold?'

Elmer looked at the river beyond their campsite and then, with a thin smile as if he'd made a decision, he made a gesture that took in the river and the route to the mountains.

'Some.'

His movement lowered his collar and revealed a long scar around his neck that Norton hadn't noticed before. When Elmer saw Norton's interest, he raised his chin, which revealed that the scar was thin with the skin being tight and ridged.

After considering the wound, Norton decided it was a rope burn.

'That looks painful,' Norton said with a gulp. 'How did that happen?'

'That's not important. What is important is that Elmer has information.' Elmer pointed upriver. 'When most prospectors reach the river fork, they go east to where the original gold rush broke out.'

'I know. That's what we did the last time.'

'Elmer has heard of a promised land to the west.'

Norton nodded. They'd decided on the way to the trading post that if they embarked on a second expedition, they'd go west. So this information made him pleased that he'd talked with Elmer, even if his odd way of speaking made him uncomfortable.

'We've heard such tales and we've followed a few.'

Elmer nodded and then stood to face the glowing campfire where the other men were sitting back and warming their hands. From his pocket he withdrew a bundle wrapped in a kerchief, which he placed on his other palm.

He walked towards the fire with the hand thrust out. His slow progress and odd posture ensured that everyone's attention was on him and then, when he stopped before the fire, was turned to the object resting on his palm.

With a deft swipe, he untied the bundle and revealed a jewel-encrusted cross that sparkled in the firelight.

'Do you have faith in Elmer's ability to lead you to

47

gold?' Elmer said.

Elmer's dark eyes were wid, suggesting that the answer to this question was more important than Norton would have expected.

'After what you did in the post,' John said, staring at the cross, 'we trust you.'

Elmer bared his teeth in a wide smile, a sight that was at odds with his impenetrable, dark eyes. An uneasy feeling in his guts made Norton sway, but the others didn't notice.

They were too busy crowding in to examine the dazzling cross.

CHAPTER 5

'You don't need his help,' Wilfred said, pausing from helping Jeff drag the comatose Dewey down the road. 'You know Elmer Drake headed to the Redemption Mountains with the prospectors.'

Jeff helped Wilfred prop Dewey up against a wall before he replied.

'I could spend my whole life roaming through those mountains and never meet another man,' he said. 'Unfortunately, I need *him*.'

Wilfred smiled. 'Only if you can sober him up enough for you to get any sense out of him.'

Jeff returned the smile, acknowledging that he'd noted Wilfred's emphasis on this being a task for him alone. While he considered Wilfred's hopeful expression, he had to admit he'd delivered more than he'd expected. It also seemed likely that, despite his evasive explanations about Maggie Cartwright's activities, he hadn't been involved in her death.

He was about to nod when someone shouted a

warning cry outside the saloon they'd just left. Wilfred craned his neck seeking out the trouble, but Jeff pointed in the opposite direction.

'Ignore that. Help me get him to the stables.'

Wilfred put a hand on Dewey's shoulder, but then withdrew it.

'And then?'

'And then. . . .' Jeff trailed off when he saw movement down the road. Four men were striding towards them. Marshal Root was leading the delegation with a hand held high in a gesture that told them to stay where they were. 'And then we get out of everyone's way real quick.'

Wilfred didn't waste time questioning him. He took one arm while Jeff took the other and they swung Dewey away from the wall before heading off down the road.

'Hey,' Root shouted behind them, 'I want that man.'

Jeff's and Wilfred's only response was to speed up and, perhaps registering the danger he was in or perhaps because the night air was sobering him up, Dewey helped himself by walking.

The stables was two buildings away when their pursuers broke into a trot. Their pattering footfalls encouraged Dewey to tear himself away from Jeff and Wilfred. He teetered until he got his balance and then, with one shoulder thrust down low, he set off at a run.

Dewey stumbled with every other pace and he skewed off into the road, but Jeff judged that he was making fast enough progress. So while Wilfred hurried on after him, he looked back.

The pursuing men had fanned out with three men stepping into the road while Root ran steadily down the boardwalk. Jeff judged that they weren't running fast enough to intercept Wilfred and Dewey before they reached the stables, so he turned away.

His confidence didn't last. When he passed the corner of the last building before coming to the stables, he saw the reason for their pursuers' steady pace.

Four men were waiting for them in the stable doorway, led by Deputy Eddie Bell. When they saw the straggling line of men approaching, they swung away from the door to form a line.

Wilfred slowed, letting Jeff catch up with him, but the inebriated Dewey carried on with his lumbering stride, forcing two men to close up to bar his way. Dewey ran on until he stumbled into them. They wrapped arms around his chest, halting him, and then hurled him backwards. He went tumbling on to his back.

Dewey sat up, shook himself, and then moved to push himself back on to his feet, but his hand failed to connect with the ground. He keeled over and lay in a crumpled heap, peering up at the line of men with his head lolling in a way that made Jeff think he was seeing at least eight men.

'Why do you want Dewey?' Jeff said, standing between the sprawling Dewey and Root.

'He's under arrest,' Root said when he'd slowed to a halt.

While Wilfred sighed with relief at Root's lack of interest in him, Jeff turned to consider the rough circle of men who now surrounded them.

'You're buzzards,' Dewey shouted, slurring his speech while waving at the men, 'circling around waiting to pick me off. Go find the dead instead.'

Dewey embarked on another attempt to gain his feet. This time he slammed down face first into the dirt, where he lay spread-eagled while waving his arms ineffectually like a beached fish.

The pathetic sight made several men look away in disgust while others looked to Root for guidance.

'Prospectors go to the mountains,' the marshal said, glaring down at Dewey with contempt. 'And many go missing, never to be seen again. Yet nobody has ever dared talk. Since your misfortune, that's changed. I now have enough to lock you away.'

Root gestured for two men to seize Dewey and those men moved towards him. Jeff blocked their way, so, with a confrontation now inevitable, Wilfred shuffled away with his hands raised and his head lowered as he avoided catching anyone's eye.

Jeff couldn't blame him, as even with his help they were too heavily outnumbered to win this battle. He spread his hands and faced the marshal. When he spoke he lowered his tone to a conciliatory one.

'Dewey's taking me to the mountains to help some prospectors.'

'The only person Dewey's ever helped is himself. Stand aside.'

'Then consider this: a fourteen-year-old girl went missing. Nobody knows if she's dead or alive. Only Dewey can help me uncover the truth about her fate.'

While Root searched Jeff's eyes, possibly seeking assurance that he was telling the truth, Jeff considered mentioning his quest to find Elmer Drake. But as the marshal probably knew that Elmer had confronted Dewey's accomplices, that probably wouldn't help him.

Root gave a slow shake of the head. 'Find someone else or join him in a cell as an accomplice.'

While Jeff wrestled with the problem he'd always known he'd face one day after deciding he'd do anything to find out what had happened to Cynthia, Wilfred screeched, making Root look at him.

What he saw made him smile. Wilfred had thrust his hands up even higher so that his arms pointed directly upwards. Then, with exaggerated movements, he made a big show of taking long paces away from Dewey and Jeff.

'This is where we go our separate ways, Jeff,' Wilfred called. 'It's been fine riding with you and I hope you don't forget everything I've done for you.'

Jeff couldn't bring himself to put Wilfred's mind at rest. Instead, he patted his pocket and felt the locket within to strengthen his resolve.

Then he raised his fists, making Root grunt with

irritation. He turned on the spot, seeking out which man would make the first move.

Unfortunately, that turned out to be everyone when, as one, the men tightened the circle. Their only concern appeared to be that they'd get in each others' way, so they darted glances at each other to coordinate their attack.

They took long paces while all Jeff could do was to move into the centre of the circle and await the onslaught. When the circle became too tight, Deputy Bell took it upon himself to attack him first. He moved in with the easy swagger of a man who was confident he'd prevail.

Jeff made him pay for being relaxed and charged him. He launched a swinging blow on the run that connected solidly with Bell's cheek and sent him reeling into the two men behind him.

All three men went down in a heap and Jeff stepped up to his next opponent. But his early good fortune ended when one of the men turned the tables on him and charged him.

The man slammed into his side and wrapped arms around his chest. His momentum carried Jeff on for three stumbling paces until he crashed into the surrounding men. Jeff went down and at least two other men fell on top of him.

He sought to raise himself, but a solid blow crashed down on his back, flattening him to the ground. Then he could only hunch his shoulders and keep his head down as he tried to limit the damage.

Glancing blows and kicks rained down on him from all directions until his attackers coordinated their assault. Someone sat down heavily on his back and grabbed the back of his head. While others thudded blows into his side and legs, this man ground his face into the dirt.

Jeff braced himself and tried to buck him. The effort felt futile, but to his surprise the weight lifted off him. He tensed, awaiting the next blow, but it didn't come. Jeff shook the dirt from his eyes and mouth and rolled over to a sitting position.

He was still surrounded by a circle of men and they were looking at Marshal Root. Jeff assumed he'd given the order to desist, but when he got a clear view of the lawman, he saw that Wilfred had moved in on Root. While everyone's attention had been on pummelling Jeff, Wilfred had disarmed the marshal and then slammed Root's own gun up against his neck.

'You've just made a big mistake,' Root said, considering Wilfred from the corner of his eye. 'You could have left unharmed. Now you'll end up in a cell with these two.'

'I'd prefer to think,' Wilfred said with more assurance than Jeff had heard him assume before, 'that you'll start being real nice to me to stop me blowing your head off.'

Wilfred ground the barrel into Root's neck, making the marshal gesture frantically at his men, ordering them to back away. The moment they took a backward pace, Jeff wasted no time in questioning his luck.

He got to his feet and batted the dust from his clothing, finding that Wilfred's timely intervention had saved him from the worst the men could have done. While fingering a developing bruise on his side, he roughly pushed a man aside whom he'd seen landing blows on him.

Then he slapped a hand on Dewey's back and dragged him up. As Dewey's eyes were rolling and he didn't appear to be aware that he was being fought over, Jeff needed to make two attempts before he got him on his feet.

Jeff slapped Dewey's cheek. When that failed to rouse him, he helped him to the stable door where he propped him up against the wall.

Dewey needed two more slaps before Jeff got a response and then it was only a murmur. So Jeff carried on, with each blow getting stronger. After five slaps, his swinging blow bent Dewey double, making Root laugh at his rough treatment.

When Jeff moved to slap him again, Dewey grabbed his hand.

'All right,' he growled. 'I heard you the first time. It's time to go.'

Jeff patted his back. Then, following Dewey's instructions, he entered the stables and found his horse. Five minutes later, he led their three horses outside to find that Wilfred had organized the group.

He was holding Root at gunpoint to the right of the door while the rest of the men stood in a line to the left. Their guns were in a pile at Wilfred's feet.

Dewey was standing unaided, one hand on his forehead, the other clutching his stomach, looking as if he were undecided as to whether he wanted to pass out or be sick.

Jeff didn't give him the time to make that decision: he helped him up into the saddle. Once seated, Dewey considered the bulging saddle-bag behind him. Jeff didn't know what was in it, but the sight cheered Dewey and, with a whoop of delight, he moved on without being asked.

As soon as he'd ridden past the line of men, Jeff gave Wilfred a quick nod of support, then mounted his horse. He held a gun on Root, letting Wilfred release his hold and hurry on to his horse.

'This doesn't end here,' Root said, stretching his neck where the gun had dug in.

'Except it could,' Jeff said in a neutral tone. He lowered his gun. 'I only want Dewey for this one mission, which will save lives, solve an old crime, and bring a man to justice. Then he's all yours.'

Root glared at Wilfred's back as he hurried on after Dewey into the gloom.

'You've got some noble aims there.' Root laughed, regaining his authority now that he was no longer being held at gunpoint. 'I hope they let you sleep easy tonight.'

The men smirked. Several men took slow paces towards Jeff while the rest edged closer to their pile of weaponry.

'I always sleep easy,' Jeff said.

He gave his gun a long look before he holstered it. Then he turned his horse towards Wilfred's receding form and, at a gallop, he rode off.

Before he reached the edge of town he glanced over his shoulder, to see that the men were strapping on their weaponry while others were going into the stables. Root was directing operations with angry gestures.

'Don't arrest them now,' he shouted, his voice echoing down the road. 'Kill them all on sight!'

CHAPTER 6

'Obliged for what you did back there,' Jeff said when he, Wilfred and Dewey had been resting up for a while.

After several detours to confuse their pursuers, they'd ridden along the rail tracks and fetched up in the entrance to Redemption Gorge. By then the moon had risen and so, as this position let them see anyone approaching from the town while the sheer rock face afforded them protection, they'd agreed to hole up for the night.

The moment they'd stopped Dewey had fallen out of the saddle. He was now propped up against the rock face and was delivering rasping snores.

'To be honest I was only saving my own skin,' Wilfred said, his grin bright in the low moonlight. He shuffled closer to sit with Jeff in the shadows. 'The way I figured it, if I ran, you'd try to keep yourself out of a cell by telling Root about me.'

'Obliged for your honesty. I would have done that.'

Wilfred sighed. 'Obliged for *your* honesty.'

The two men sat in silence, listening to the light wind. To his relief, Jeff heard no signs of pursuit.

'But no matter what happens now,' Jeff said, 'I won't tell Root about your past.'

Jeff expected an exuberant reaction, but Wilfred only looked at the plains.

'Root could arrive at any moment and shoot us up. So I reckon we have to stay together for a while longer.'

'Or then again, splitting up might give us both a better chance of getting away.'

Wilfred started to reply, but then a stray noise in the night, perhaps a night animal scurrying near by, silenced him. He glared into the dark until, after gulping loudly, he shook his head.

'I'm not going nowhere on my own right now.'

Jeff released a long sigh. 'You've spent our every moment together waiting for me to declare our bargain complete so that you can go. Now the moment I let you go, you want to stay with me.'

Wilfred shrugged. 'If we survive the night, ask me again in the morning.'

Jeff smiled. So, with their next actions decided, he took up a position closer to the rail tracks, where he looked out for Root.

A few minutes later the noise that had worried Wilfred sounded again. This time it was clearly a footfall crunching on grit. Both men peered into the gloom, but when Jeff discerned a form approaching, it was smaller than Root's; it was coming from deeper into the gorge, and it wore a habit.

'Sister Angelica,' Jeff called in case Wilfred hadn't recognized her.

The nun came closer and cast upon him a harsh glare that made him think that meeting Marshal Root would have been less disconcerting.

'Why are you men skulking around in the dark?' she demanded.

'We were resting up for a while,' Jeff said.

'Running away from trouble more like.' She smiled thinly when Wilfred coughed in embarrassment. 'And most likely you're running from Marshal Root, not that it's hard to avoid him. But whatever your need, the hospitality of the sisters of the Sacred Cross is always available.'

She pointed further up the gorge. Although Jeff reckoned a night on the cold and hard ground might be preferable, he nodded.

So, with Wilfred holding Dewey up they followed her for around 200 yards to a small building set to the side of the gorge. As it was hemmed in by high rocks on three sides, Jeff reckoned they could have easily ridden by without noticing it.

Angelica directed them inside and then to an unfurnished annex in the cruciform-shaped hospital. The building here was incomplete and the large room lacked a roof.

A silent nun, her head bowed, was waiting to serve them. Angelica identified her as Sister Verena and

61

then looked them over with the same level of disdain as she'd shown Root.

'I'm grateful for your help,' Jeff said.

'I'm grateful too,' Wilfred said. He removed his hat, although unfortunately he released his tight hold of Dewey's shoulders. The drunken man dropped to the floor. 'And so is he.'

'I've often said that no man is beyond redemption,' Angelica said, staring down at Dewey. 'In his case I may have to change my opinion.'

Verena shuffled on the spot, perhaps acknowledging that Angelica didn't change her mind very often.

Jeff smiled. 'Dewey's helping me with an important—'

'I'm sure it's not important, but no matter. You're welcome to shelter for the night and, if you need anything, Sister Verena will be on duty.' Angelica glanced up at the night sky. 'We've been short-handed since Mark went missing and I'm afraid the work on the hospital isn't complete, but we're here to serve without asking for anything in return.'

'Obliged,' Jeff said.

As they waited for the nuns to leave, the group stood in silence, except for Dewey's rasping snores, until Angelica raised her heels to get closer to Jeff's eye-level.

'As I said,' she said, her raised voice echoing in the room, 'I'm afraid the work on the hospital isn't complete, but we're here to serve without asking for anything in return.'

Jeff snorted a laugh, then fished in his pocket. With practised speed the offered coins disappeared into Angelica's habit, after which she led Verena away, leaving the three men to settle down for the night.

Jeff and Wilfred agreed that they'd sleep in a corner of the room, figuring that they would hear Root if he came to the hospital. Within minutes Wilfred drifted off to sleep, but Jeff stayed alert for another hour. In that time he heard only a door opening and closing several times, and once a man called out for Verena, the strained tone suggesting he was one of the sick people the nuns tended.

Feeling more relaxed, Jeff dropped off to sleep. He didn't stir until Wilfred prodded him awake at first light. Dewey, when he'd been shaken awake, couldn't remember much about what had happened on the previous night, but he did remember the deal he'd made: to take them to where the prospectors and Elmer Drake had gone.

Wilfred reported that he himself hadn't changed his mind overnight about their splitting up. So they went to the main door and looked outside. They could see nobody, not even the sisters, so, before Angelica could have a chance to waylay them, they slipped away.

The sun was poking above the horizon when they led their horses out of the gorge. The plains leading to Redemption were clearly to be seen. So, following Dewey's terse directions, they set off for the distant

Redemption Mountains, as so many other hopeful prospectors had done before them.

They lined up, with Dewey at the front and Jeff at the back, from where he could watch the other two men when he wasn't looking over his shoulder for Root. But the day passed without incident and by late afternoon they closed on the river alongside which they had tracked yesterday.

As the sun lowered and the burnt-out wreck came into view ahead, Dewey dropped back to ride beside Jeff for the first time.

'There's plenty of these around,' he said. 'People come out here looking for gold. They don't find it. They do find death.'

'I'd heard as much from Root. And he thought you were responsible.' Jeff waited, but Dewey gave only a bored shrug. 'So how much further are we travelling together?'

Dewey pointed upriver. 'After another three days' riding, two rivers join up to make this one. I gather the prospectors explored the east fork, but people trying their luck for a second time usually explore the west fork. That never works either.'

Dewey chuckled, suggesting he had good reason to be sure about their movements but that he wasn't prepared to divulge how he knew.

'And where do we go then?'

Dewey's brief good mood ended and, with a hand that had a slight tremor, he rubbed his neck.

'I'll take you to some places where these people

usually try.' He gulped. 'But as we agreed, when we pick up on their trail for sure, you're on your own. I'm not going nowhere near a dead man again.'

Jeff considered questioning Dewey about why he had been convinced that Elmer had died, but he figured Dewey wasn't the type to answer questions freely. As they'd have other opportunities to talk before he left them, Jeff pointed back over his shoulder.

'Are you forgetting Root is on our tail?'

Dewey didn't even look back. 'I haven't. I'd sooner die at his hands with my soul intact.'

Jeff nodded after which Dewey reverted to silence. Later, two miles on from the wreck, they settled down for the night.

They took it in turns to keep watch. This time Dewey did his fair share, but despite everyone's concern about the dangers that were following on behind and those that awaited them ahead, the night passed quietly, as did the next two days and nights.

They followed Dewey's instructions by branching off at the river fork, at which point he pointed out the area ahead for which he reckoned the prospectors would make tracks.

They could see for miles ahead to the mountains, which were blue-tinged and inviting from such a distance. They could also see for miles behind them and there was no sign of Root in pursuit.

This didn't surprise Jeff. They had made good time in reaching the fork and he reckoned they should have got well ahead of the marshal. From here, they would be exploring and Root would close on them, but despite this Dewey's mood was more positive than Jeff had expected after his performance in the saloon.

On the fifth night of their journey Jeff found out the reason why Dewey was relaxed and why that attitude wouldn't last for long.

Jeff awoke from a troubled sleep in which his only memory of Elmer had intruded into his dreams, to find the night air was colder than it had been at any point on their journey. Shivering he went to fetch another blanket. He saw Dewey sitting up against a rock, working his way through a bottle of whiskey.

'You never said you had liquor,' Jeff said, standing over him.

'It's none of your business,' Dewey said, slurring his words and not meeting Jeff's eye. 'My saddle-bags are mine.'

'They are.' Jeff glanced at the open saddle-bag at Dewey's side. One full bottle was poking out. 'But that explains where you got your courage to lead us this far.'

Dewey waved a dismissive hand at him, sloshing the remaining whiskey in the bottle.

'Don't judge me. There's nothing worse than the dead rising up to drag you back to hell.'

Jeff leaned forward and drew the silver locket from his pocket. He dangled it until Dewey's inebriated gaze followed its progress.

'There is. Think what it'd be like to be a fourteen-year-old girl seeing Elmer slaughter her whole family.'

Dewey gulped. Then, with a quick gesture, he put the bottle to his lips for a long swallow.

'You don't know nothing until you've faced the dark-eyed one.'

Jeff sneered with disgust. 'Maybe you're right, but after I've faced him, I won't live my life in a bottle. And soon, you'll know what that feels like because you'll have drunk all your courage.'

Dewey said nothing and so Jeff collected his blanket. It took him a while to warm up, by which time Dewey was rasping out contented snores, but Jeff found sleep hard to come by.

Every time he closed his eyes he saw Elmer standing in the doorway of his parents' home with his dark eyes set on him. Unlike the first time he'd had this recollection, Elmer was smiling.

'Is Elmer back yet?' Norton asked when he returned to their campsite.

John and Oscar both shook their heads before they joined him in peering upriver.

'Albert said they had plenty of places to search today,' John said. 'So I wouldn't get worried yet.'

Norton laughed. 'You wouldn't get worried if twenty bandits came riding towards us.'

John joined him in laughing. Then they exchanged information on what each man had found today. As usual, that was nothing.

Sadly, although Elmer claimed to have information on where they would find gold, they needed to search a large area to find the exact spot.

'But what about you?' John asked when they'd finished their reports. 'Are you worried?'

John's guarded tone and the brief glance he cast at Oscar showed that they'd been talking about something before Norton had returned and that this matter was important to them.

'You mean about Elmer?' Norton asked, his immediate response making both men smile.

Everyone having relaxed the three men sat on the edge of the water, from where they would be able to see Albert and Elmer returning.

'We've been talking about him,' Oscar said, keeping his voice low even though they were alone.

'And,' John said, 'we've both admitted we've had second thoughts about letting him join us.'

'You're wrong,' Norton said. He didn't explain until both men stared at him. 'They're first thoughts. We never actually asked him to come along.'

'I said that was the way it happened,' Oscar said, shaking a fist. He looked at John until he nodded. 'He just came along and we were all too pleased about what he'd done to object.'

Everyone frowned and sat silently until Norton made the obvious point.

'We can't change what's happened, but if we all agree, we can have that discussion with him now.'

'We have to,' Oscar said. 'He's trouble. He speaks oddly. He looks at you oddly. He has a rope burn around his neck that didn't get there by no accident, I'm sure. He always packs a gun and the holster's shiny with use. Worst of all, he doesn't know nothing about this area and we'd have just as much chance of finding gold on our own.'

After that speech John could only nod. Norton leaned closer to Oscar.

'Are you volunteering to tell him?' he asked.

Oscar's mouth fell open with shock until he saw that Norton was smiling.

'No,' he said, mustering a thin smile, 'but I'll volunteer you to tell him he can go.'

While both Oscar and Norton sat in silent contemplation of this difficult task, John looked from one to the other, his pensive expression acknowledging that, as he was the unofficial leader of the group, this duty would fall on him.

'Moving on without him,' he said, using the level tone he employed when he'd reached a decision, 'will make us all feel safer, and so. . . .'

John trailed off and pointed upriver. Norton turned to see that Elmer was making his slow way towards them.

The three men cast worried glances at each other in anticipation of the confrontation to come. Then they stood to await Elmer. They all became agitated when it became clear he was returning alone.

'Where's Albert?' Oscar called.

Elmer walked on at an unhurried pace. He said nothing until he reached them, where he considered them in his usual distracted way, as if their presence was of no more interest to him than the rocks beneath his feet.

'Failure annoyed him,' he said. 'Other journeys await.'

'You mean,' John said, 'he's decided to leave?'

Elmer didn't answer; he moved to walk past them, but Norton blocked his way, making Elmer narrow his eyes, although he did stop.

'Albert's already gone,' Elmer said. He held an arm out and swept his hand in a long arc that gave a representation of his travelling a great distance. 'That's unfortunate for him.'

Norton gulped, expecting the worst but knowing he still had to ask the obvious question.

'Why?'

'Because Elmer has found the promised land.' Elmer stilled his hand with it pointed at a bluff that was set back from the water. 'The gold is close.'

Despite the bad news about Albert, John and Oscar whooped with joy as their willingness to have a confrontation evaporated. But Norton turned away to look upriver, hoping he might catch a glimpse of Albert as he made off.

Elmer also ignored the celebrations and joined him in looking, but he set his gaze higher than the spot he'd indicated, on a place in the heavens where there wasn't even a single cloud.

Then he clasped his hands together and assumed a posture that made him look as if he were praying.

CHAPTER 7

After suffering an unsettled night, Jeff was grateful that the new day brought plenty of activity with which to occupy his mind.

For the first time they used Dewey's knowledge of the area to explore tributaries that emptied into the main river. They found signs that people had been here, but not recently.

With each failure Dewey's mood became sourer and so did Wilfred's, but Jeff became more content. He was familiar with this process. To him, every failure only eliminated one more place where his quarry wasn't to be found, making it more likely that they would find him in the next place they looked.

As it turned out, they had no success that day. Before they settled down for the night Jeff checked Dewey's saddle-bag when he wasn't looking. He was down to his last bottle.

In the morning, Dewey was edgy, suggesting that he'd drank most of the bottle during the previous night. So, reckoning that Dewey's time with them would end soon, either by his running away or by his becoming uncooperative, Jeff pressed on quickly while questioning him relentlessly about what he knew about the area.

They passed six tributaries and searched the two that Dewey claimed were used by prospectors. These helpful observations, which speeded up the search process, made Jeff hope that the end of the whiskey wouldn't mark the end of Dewey's usefulness.

With sundown an hour away, they were returning to the main river, where they planned to settle down for the night, when they encountered the first sign of people having been here recently.

Sadly, it came in the form of a body floating down the river.

Wilfred fished a branch out of the water. Then he and Jeff used it to snag the body's clothing and drag it to the side. When they laid it down on the ground, the shredded and bloodied clothing showed that this man had died a savage death.

'How long?' Wilfred asked.

'Can't tell for sure,' Jeff said. 'But he died recently, perhaps within a day.'

His guess made everyone look upriver, but nobody was visible. They still huddled closer together than they had previously, although when Dewey examined the body, he laughed.

'That man was with Elmer Drake,' he declared, slapping a raised thigh. He kicked the body in the ribs and then leaned over it. 'You didn't get to gloat for long, did you, before he sent you to hell?'

'Maybe he didn't,' Jeff said, 'but this means we're close to our quarry. If Elmer's as formidable as you claim, you have nothing to gloat about either.'

The seriousness of the situation killed off Dewey's good mood. With a final kick into the body's ribs, he hurried over to his saddle-bag. As Jeff expected, it contained only empty bottles. Dewey still found enough dregs in each bottle before he threw it aside to give him a few sips and so bolster his courage that he could confront him.

'You're the only one who'll get close to him,' he declared. He pointed at the body. 'That body says I'm going no further.'

Dewey picked up his saddle-bag. Then he took several backward steps to move closer to his horse while clutching the bag to his chest, as if it could somehow save him from whatever misfortunes awaited him.

'You're staying and helping me find Elmer,' Jeff said. 'You can't live the rest of your life as a liquor-sodden yellow-belly.'

'I'm not,' Dewey said, although when his next step kicked a bottle aside and sent it rattling over the rocks, that claim didn't sound convincing. 'But I only take on men that stay dead.'

'Why were you so sure Elmer died?'

Dewey watched the bottle until it halted, then he considered Jeff. He gave a long sigh, suggesting that he wouldn't speak, but then in a rush he barked out his explanation.

'Marshal Root was right about me. Four of us used to come out here and waylay prospectors, but we only took their gold. We never killed nobody.' He shrugged. 'It was bad for business.'

'I believe you.'

'Then a new man arrived and he muscled in on our business. He used to ride along with the prospectors and gain their trust. Then he killed them. As nobody ever lived to tell the tale, Root blamed us.'

'And that new man was Elmer?'

'Yeah. Six months ago we decided to deal with him ourselves. We laid a trap, roped him up like a steer, and hanged him. Then we dragged him along until the rope broke. We left his carcass for the buzzards.'

'But you didn't check he was dead?'

'We didn't need to. He was dead!'

Dewey waved a dismissive hand at Jeff, and then rooted around in his bag, seemingly preferring to think that a dead man had returned rather than accept that he had made a mistake. He spent so long searching for whatever he wanted that Jeff looked at Wilfred.

'Dewey's staying with me,' Jeff said. 'But you can go now.'

Wilfred said nothing and Jeff turned back to find that Dewey was smiling. Then Jeff saw the outline of a gun in his hand. It was poking against the inside of the saddle-bag.

'You're not giving the orders no more,' Dewey said. He thrust the gun barrel forward a mite to ensure that Jeff knew it was aimed at his chest. 'But you do get to die here. And I'll make sure you're dead.'

Jeff turned away slightly so that Dewey wouldn't see him inch his hand towards his holster. This let him catch a glimpse of movement from the corner of his eye. He directed his gaze away from Dewey's gun to see that Wilfred had drawn the six-shooter he'd taken off Marshal Root.

Wilfred aimed the gun skywards until he had Jeff's and Dewey's attention. Then slowly he lowered it, but he aimed for a point midway between the two men.

'Settle this between you,' Wilfred said with a smirk. 'Then I'll kill whoever survives.'

'Why?' Jeff snapped. 'I said you could go.'

Dewey looked at Wilfred and, in his befuddled state, without the liquor to fuel his courage, he swung the gun's aim away from Jeff's chest. As this left Jeff with only one man to worry about he edged his hand closer to his holster.

Wilfred firmed his jaw, looking as if he wouldn't reply, but the temptation to gloat proved too great.

'When Elmer Drake was at the post,' he said, 'the owner saw that he had a jewel-encrusted cross. Soon, it'll be mine.'

'Nobody would take on Elmer unless they'd got themselves a death wish,' Dewey said. He grinned wildly. 'But a valuable cross like that would make it worth the risk.'

After Wilfred's revelation, the three men sized each other up. Jeff reckoned he could dispose of Dewey easily and, as Wilfred wasn't watching Dewey carefully, it appeared that he expected that result too. For his part, Dewey looked at both men nervously as if he were sure he wouldn't survive.

'If I die here,' Jeff said, talking quietly, 'whichever one of you survives will surely die at Elmer's hands. But if you let me live, I'll get Elmer while you two can share the cross. Jewels don't matter none to me, just Elmer.'

Doubt flashed in Wilfred's eyes while Dewey's gaze strayed to the empty bottles.

'Perhaps we should make a deal,' Dewey said with a gulp. 'Jeff gets the man. We share the cross.'

'We?' Wilfred murmured with a sly smile that promised that, no matter what they agreed here, other battles would be fought later.

'Yeah,' Dewey said, regaining the usual truculence in his voice. He lowered the bag to reveal the gun, although the flap caught the barrel and aimed it downwards. 'We agree that we join forces to find Elmer and then we two share what we get.'

'All right,' Wilfred said with a guarded tone. 'That sounds—'

Wilfred dropped to the ground. A strangulated gasp died on his lips while the gun fell from his hand and his other hand rose to his bloodied chest. A moment later a gunshot sounded behind Jeff and, with an instinctive reaction, he turned at the hip while drawing his gun.

He faced a rock-strewn slope, many of those rocks being large enough for the shooter to have taken refuge behind one of them. The slope led on to the sheer rock face of a bluff 200 yards away.

Jeff went to one knee and kept still while he looked for movement. After thirty seconds of silence, Dewey sidled into position beside him where he lay on his chest with his gun thrust forward.

'You look to the bluff,' Dewey said from the corner of his mouth as if the confrontation of the last few minutes had never taken place. 'I'll cover the river side.'

'And Wilfred?'

'He won't be no use.'

Jeff nodded. 'Elmer Drake or Marshal Root?'

'We're still alive. So that means it's the lawman.'

Jeff considered Dewey. For once his hands were steady and his gaze was resolute, although Jeff couldn't tell whether that was because he was thinking about claiming the cross or because they were confronting Root and not Elmer.

Then, with the duplicitous Dewey covering his back, Jeff waited for whoever was out there to come for them.

CHAPTER 8

'Albert wouldn't leave without talking to us first,' Oscar said for not the first time during the last twenty-four hours.

'I know,' Norton said. 'We've been a team for three years. Something has to be wrong.'

Both men looked at John for his response and, in acceptance of the seriousness of the situation, John took a while to reply.

Today Elmer had led them up the side of a bluff to the place where he claimed they'd find gold.

Everyone's excitement had kept their doubts at bay right up until the moment they'd stood on the rocky ground set back from the bluff. It had looked no different from the many other stretches of rocky ground that they'd explored for the last three months.

For the rest of the day they'd rooted around, but they'd done so only half-heartedly while they kept one eye on Elmer. This was the first time he'd

wandered out of earshot, after which the three men
had wasted no time in huddling to discuss him.

'Something is wrong,' John said with more assurance than Norton had ever heard from him before.
'And this time I'll find out what it is. Elmer's not dis-
tracting us no more with his tales of gold.'

The three men all nodded, each nod making
everyone look even more determined. Then, with a
coordinated move, they swung round, aiming to
march off and confront Elmer. However, while they'd
been talking, he'd disappeared from view.

They all shot narrow-eyed glances at each other, as
if this proved that something was amiss. Without
further discussion they walked over to their pile of
belongings.

Two minutes later each of the three men had a six-
shooter at his hip for the first time that Norton could
remember.

With the comforting weight adding a roll to his
stride, he set off for the last place he'd seen Elmer.
Oscar and John walked a few paces behind him.

Norton walked towards the side of a large, round
boulder, this being the most likely place for Elmer to
have gone. Twenty yards from the boulder he saw
Elmer, but he was doing nothing untoward.

He was looking beyond the edge of the bluff that
was set between them and the river. He raised a hand
in a gesture that told Norton to stop, although he
didn't look in Norton's direction.

Norton did as ordered, making Oscar and John

close up behind him. Then Elmer gestured for them to approach slowly.

'What's wrong?' Norton asked.

'Visitors,' Elmer said, 'and they're trouble. Listen.'

He put a hand to his ear. A few seconds later a gunshot tore out, the sound coming from below them at the bottom of the bluff.

Norton and his friends took no chances; they dropped to their knees and looked around them.

Elmer raised an ear and even sniffed the air. Then he pointed forward and set off, walking purposefully towards the direction of the noise.

'He may be odd,' Oscar said, speaking quietly, 'but he sure doesn't avoid trouble.'

'Yeah,' Norton said reluctantly. 'Perhaps we should postpone confronting him until we find out what this is about.'

He spoke quietly too, but almost as if he'd heard him, Elmer stopped and looked back.

Since he did not move on they joined him. Then the four men lined up and walked towards the top of the bluff.

Twenty yards from the edge they lowered their heads. They crawled and then snaked across the ground until they reached the edge.

Elmer looked down briefly before drawing back his head so that the men below couldn't see him. He didn't explain what he'd seen as Norton shuffled forward on his belly to lie beside him.

Below was the rocky ground beside the river. On the gentle slope that led to the bottom of the bluff, one man had taken cover behind a large boulder while several other men were scurrying along a dried-out rill.

They were planning to ambush two men who were fifty yards away. After Norton had peered at them for a minute, he observed that a third man was lying on his back. He wasn't moving.

Norton dropped down from view and shuffled back from the edge to report his findings.

'We have to help them,' John said immediately.

'But which ones?' Oscar said. 'We don't know who's in the right here.'

'Eight men are moving in on two,' Norton said. 'I reckon that tells us everything we need to know.'

'Yeah,' Oscar murmured, 'that we probably can't do nothing to help the two.'

Norton considered each man in turn. Their glazed expressions and their failure to meet his eye showed that, like him, they were contemplating turning their backs on this situation. His gaze rested finally on Elmer, and the man's formidable physique and the memory of what he'd done in the trading post gave Norton heart.

'The trouble is,' he said, 'we could be their next targets. So I reckon we should make the first move.'

Elmer said nothing, but John and Oscar gave reluctant nods.

'And what is that move?' Oscar asked.

'You two outflank the attackers.' Norton pointed along the top of the bluff, indicating the route they should take. 'Elmer and I will see how many we can pick off from up here.'

John and Oscar smiled. Then they moved off without complaint, although Norton couldn't tell whether that was because they agreed with his suggestion or were relieved because they didn't have to stay with Elmer.

When the two men had moved on for fifty yards and were seeking out a route down the bluff that would keep them hidden from below, Norton shuffled back to the edge.

Elmer joined him to look down at a scene that had developed in the last few minutes.

The two defenders were lying on their chests, facing their attackers, who had settled into their final positions. Three men were hiding behind boulders while the men in the rill knelt at twenty-yard intervals.

Elmer shuffled away from the edge, sat up and rooted through his pockets. He removed a book and, with his eyes closed, he laid a hand on the cover. With a snort of surprise, Norton saw that it was a Bible.

'Your gun will be more use than that,' Norton said when Elmer opened his eyes.

'This,' Elmer said, tapping the book, 'gives Elmer all the protection he needs.'

'That may give Elmer everything he needs,'

Norton murmured, 'but what about you?'

Norton hadn't meant his question to be taken seriously, having spoken out of surprise at seeing what was in Elmer's pocket, but Elmer's dark eyes opened wide.

It may have been because they were facing the arc of light on the western horizon, but the eyes appeared lighter than they usually did. Elmer even smiled in an easy way that didn't make Norton feel queasy.

'This will explain.' Elmer flicked through the book. It fell open at a well-thumbed page, which he turned round for Norton to read.

Over Elmer's shoulder, Norton saw John and Oscar slipping over the edge of the bluff, but despite the urgency of the situation he shuffled closer to Elmer.

Elmer had indicated a passage in the Gospel of Mark and the intense way he studied Norton's posture made it appear that his reaction was important.

Norton read a section in which a paralysed man was first forgiven and then cured. He couldn't see what had interested Elmer and so he shook his head.

'I don't understand,' he said.

Elmer lowered his eyelids until they half-covered his eyes. Then with a slow reverential movement he closed the book and slipped it back in his pocket.

'Which is as it should be,' Elmer said in a benevolent way, as if he were explaining something obvious to a child. He lowered his collar to feel the ridge of scar tissue around his neck. 'Have you not faith in Elmer yet?'

Elmer had asked Norton something like this once before and, bearing in mind his earlier conversation with his friends, Norton reckoned he should tell the truth.

'No,' he said.

Elmer nodded. The two men considered each other until a gunshot ripped out below and shattered the silence. It was the first shot to have been fired since the one that had attracted their attention.

Elmer lowered his eyelids the rest of the way down. He moved to the edge of the bluff.

Then, almost as if it were an afterthought, he swung back, his eyes snapping open and his fist rising up.

He and Norton were keeping low, so Elmer couldn't put much force behind the blow, but it still crunched into Norton's chin and sent him spinning.

Norton came to rest on his chest where, with a shake of the head, he slapped both hands to the ground. He pushed himself up while moving away from Elmer, which reduced the impact of a second swiping punch to the side of the head.

The glancing blow still made him roll over and landed him on his side on the edge of the bluff.

When his vision stopped swirling he looked down the sheer drop and saw that the attackers were advancing, with gunfire accompanying every movement. He shuffled away from the edge to find that Elmer was looming over him.

As Elmer remained standing in full view of the gunfighters below, Norton stayed still, feeling unsure how he should react to such reckless behaviour, but Elmer smiled in an apparently unconcerned manner.

Then he kicked out. The toe of his boot slipped under Norton's side. Elmer flipped him over with a quick motion.

The kick was so strong that Norton was sure he was airborne before he dropped down. Then, with a lurch of his stomach, he saw the edge of the bluff pass by as he embarked on a longer drop down to the solid ground a hundred feet below.

Without much hope he thrust out a hand and, to his relief, it smacked down on a rock.

He gripped the rock while his left hand found scrambling purchase in the looser dirt on the edge. Then his chest slapped against the rock face and, with his breath held, he fetched up with his arms outstretched and his feet dangling.

When he was sure he wouldn't fall any further he sought a ledge on which he could rest, but his boots only scraped ineffectually against the smooth rock as they failed to find purchase.

Then he had another problem to deal with when Elmer appeared above him.

As blasts of gunfire tore out below, coming from different directions, Elmer stood with his hands on his hips seemingly oblivious to the danger while he surveyed the scene in his usual distracted way. Then he considered Norton's predicament.

He noted his right hand holding on around a rock and the left hand digging into the dirt on the edge. Then he leaned forward to consider the sheer drop below him.

Elmer winked at him.

Then he walked away.

CHAPTER 9

'We've got help,' Dewey said.

'We'll need it,' Jeff said, peering in the direction Dewey had indicated. 'The prospectors?'

'I don't know. I can't see them yet.' Dewey continued peering at the bluff, but then his smile died and he turned to Jeff. 'If it is, Elmer Drake will be helping them.'

Jeff shrugged. 'Right now I'll settle for help from anyone.'

Earlier, they'd seen enough to confirm that Marshal Root was leading a group of men of around the same size as the group they'd defied in Redemption.

Surrounded, heavily outnumbered and with little cover, Jeff reckoned that their only chance was to hold out until darkness came and then sneak away.

Root appeared to be aware of the urgency of taking them without delay, for his men had come closer. Jeff's and Dewey's only cover was the depression in which they'd made camp, and between them and Root was a stretch of flat ground with little cover.

But now someone was firing at Root's men from the bluff, sowing consternation as they aimed at their unguarded backs. Jeff ran his gaze along the bluff until he saw their helpers.

Two men were on a ledge halfway down the bluff while a third man was moving towards them. A fourth man was attempting to climb down the steepest part of the bluff although, after Jeff had watched him for a few moments, he decided he was in fact dangling over a sheer drop.

Root's group started firing at this man, but he was out of their firing range and puffs of dust went up along the rock face some distance from where he was struggling. But they were sure to get in a lucky shot eventually, and his colleagues were helping him by laying down continual gunfire.

A cry of pain went up as these men had their first success and a moment later one of Root's men stood up in the rill with his back arched before he dropped to the ground.

'We need to act now while we have a chance,' Dewey said in a commanding voice that made Jeff pause before replying that even though he agreed, he wasn't following Dewey's orders.

'While they're distracted, head that way,' he said. He pointed at a small mound, one of the few places that afforded cover. 'I'll go the other way.'

Dewey considered the slightly larger mound that Jeff had picked for himself and, although it was further away and closer to Root's position, he shook his head.

'We go together,' Dewey muttered. Then he flashed a smile confirming that he knew he'd erred. 'If we survive, we can argue about who's in charge later.'

Jeff was minded to have that argument now, but after a brief lull, a rapid burst of gunfire broke out and another of Root's men stumbled into view. He swayed to one side while trying to feel his back, then fell over the boulder he'd been hiding behind. He lay still, with his arms dangling.

Jeff put his concerns about Dewey's recent behaviour from his mind and jumped to his feet. Bent double, he set off at a run for the mound.

Dewey followed. As they pounded across the ground, Jeff looked along the various positions where Root's men had gone to ground.

Other than the men on the ledge, he couldn't see anyone and, while these men laid down steady gunfire, Jeff added to the confusion by shooting on the run. At his heels Dewey joined in and the two men splayed wild gunfire to either side.

Neither man picked out any targets, but they reached the mound without mishap. There they threw themselves on to their chests and peered over the top.

Three of their helpers had now come together on the ledge, where they were keeping low, so that Jeff could see only their heads. The fourth man had now found a resting place on the rock face.

Root's group exchanged muttered comments and although Jeff couldn't hear the words, the tone sounded worried. The result of the debate came when Root bobbed up for a moment from behind the boulder he'd been hiding behind.

'Call your men off,' he shouted before ducking down again. 'Every shot you take against a lawman and his legally sworn-in posse only makes this worse for you.'

'They're not my men,' Jeff shouted. 'But we will defend ourselves.'

'In that case Dewey Shark's not leaving here alive and neither will his accomplices.'

Despite his threat, and perhaps after seeing how close Jeff and Dewey were, Root got to his feet and, with his head down, he hurried back to the rill where most of his men were.

Jeff still hoped they could talk Root round, so he let him go without reprisal, but after the marshal had taken several strides, Dewey swung his gun up. Jeff moved to slap his gun hand down, but he reacted too slowly and Dewey loosed a quick and deadly shot that ripped into the lawman's back.

Root dropped to his knees. He twisted so that he stared at them with his mouth opening to shout something. Then he keeled over on to his front with the comment unsaid.

Another man appeared from behind the boulder and made as if to go to his aid. Dewey's rapid gunfire made him scurry back. Then a well-aimed shot from high on the ledge made sure he didn't reach safety.

Cries of consternation went up from various positions as news of Root's demise was passed from man to man. Then silence reigned.

Jeff kept his thoughts to himself about Dewey's action. Wordlessly he exchanged glances with him, as they silently debated what they thought the group would do now.

The answer came when sustained gunfire burst out from one position, the men having clearly grouped up. All of the fire was aimed up at the ledge and designed to cover a hasty retreat.

Jeff and Dewey hurried them on their way with quick shots and then ducked down. When Jeff next looked up, Deputy Bell was leading the survivors along the base of the bluff with hardly a backwards glance. Jeff counted only four men.

'Seems we've prevailed,' Jeff said, getting to his feet.

'Root made a big mistake when he tangled with us,' Dewey said with a grin, the euphoria of their survival clearly making him forget that they'd be dead if they hadn't had help.

'And you made a big mistake,' Jeff said, 'when you killed a lawman and made us both wanted men.'

Dewey frowned. Then, acting cautiously by walking sideways, he moved on to Root. While he was confirming that the lawman was dead, Jeff edged his way past the boulder. He found two more bodies and then moved on to the rill, in which he saw another dead man.

'We already were,' Dewey said joining him. 'At least now we get to live for long enough to escape, thanks to our friends up there.'

Jeff looked up the side of the bluff. He was now close enough to discern the predicament of one of the men. He had found refuge on a thin ledge and he was attempting to climb back up to the top. The other men were staying down.

Now that the gunfight was over Jeff turned his thoughts to their helpers' identities. If the body they'd found in the water had come from this group, they made up the right numbers to be the prospectors he and Dewey were searching for.

Jeff pointed up to the ledge. 'Let's go and thank our new friends.'

Dewey nodded and set off. Jeff let him lead. Dewey readily found a route up an incline that wasn't as steep as the one that was giving the other man problems.

Bearing in mind his concerns about who these people were, Jeff let Dewey reach them first. Dewey was ten yards higher than Jeff was when he clambered up on to the ledge.

What Dewey saw there made him come to a sudden halt. He looked around nervously before beckoning Jeff to hurry.

It turned out that their defenders had paid a heavy price for helping them. Two of the three men lay unmoving, face down. The third man wasn't here.

Dewey knelt between the two prone figures and raised their heads. He gave a quick smile before he looked up at Jeff, shaking his head.

'They're the prospectors Elmer helped at the trading post.' His tone was low and he seemed disconcerted.

'Decided not to gloat this time?'

Dewey pointed at the red holes in their backs with a shaking hand, then rolled them both over to confirm that they had no other wounds.

'Yeah, because unless Root shot them both in the back from down there, the third man killed them.'

Jeff gulped as, like Dewey, he accepted the likely chain of events that had led to their deaths. He swung round to look up to the top of the bluff.

'And that third man is Elmer Drake,' he murmured.

'And you can't kill a dead man.'

Dewey's shaking tone suggested that his recently found confidence was about to evaporate. Jeff pointed along the length of the bluff.

'Help that other man. I'll get Elmer.'

He didn't wait for Dewey to agree. Keeping his head down, he scrambled up to the top of the bluff and peered over the edge.

A hundred yards on a man was moving away. He walked at an unhurried pace until he disappeared behind a large boulder.

Jeff recalled the only sighting he had had of

Elmer, but the picture in his mind wasn't good enough for him to confirm this man was his quarry.

He set off, running without caution, and reached the boulder quickly. Then he slowed and worked his way round it.

The man was still walking. He was now fifty yards away and heading along the bottom of an expanse of loose scree. He would disappear behind a crag within a minute, so Jeff let him move on unchallenged.

He took the opportunity to check on Dewey's progress. To his surprise, Dewey was doing as he'd been ordered and he was working his way along the top of the bluff. Jeff also noted that these people's campsite was beyond the boulder, along with their horses, but his quarry was moving away.

This observation cheered him, so the moment the man went out of his view he ran after him. As before he slowed only when he reached the point where the man had disappeared.

He saw a boulder ten yards ahead. He took refuge behind it and peered over the top.

The man was sitting on a flat rock thirty yards away behind the remnants of an old fire, looking down towards the distant river. Slowly he turned to Jeff. His dark eyes considered him.

'Stop skulking about,' he said, 'and show Elmer who's there.'

On hearing his quarry's identity confirmed, Jeff gulped and looked skywards for a moment, enjoying his relief at finally ending his quest.

Then he considered his chances if he were to just leap up and take a shot at Elmer.

Elmer wore a gun at his hip, but Jeff reckoned he could get in a shot before he reached it. That wouldn't get him the answers he needed, and so he rose to his feet.

'I'm Jeff Dale,' he said.

'Is that supposed to mean something to Elmer?'

Jeff came out from behind the boulder and walked towards Elmer. He dangled his hands loosely with his right hand never straying far from his holster.

'The fact that you don't remember my family name suggests that many others have met the fate of those prospectors and Maggie Cartwright . . . and the Harris family back in Dirtwood.'

'And which of those unfortunates concerns you?'

Jeff drew the locket from his pocket and held it up. Elmer considered it, then met his gaze with his dark eyes.

'That would be the property of the girl who was once known as Cynthia.'

'Yes,' Jeff breathed although Elmer hadn't phrased his statement as a question.

'And your connection to her would be that you were childhood sweethearts.' Again the comment hadn't been phrased as a question, and this time Jeff didn't respond. 'And so you've been searching for Elmer for ten years, looking to make him suffer.'

'You're not that important,' Jeff spat. 'Everybody forgot about you years ago. Only the girl matters now.'

Jeff drew the locket back into his left hand and slipped it into his breast pocket. At the same time he moved his right hand down to rest beside his holster.

His motion didn't appear to concern Elmer, as Jeff still kept his hand away from his hip. Then Elmer slapped his legs as if he'd made a decision.

From his pocket he removed a jewelled cross, presumably the one that had interested Wilfred.

'Then this matter should end here.' Elmer stood with the cross resting on a palm and aimed at him.

Jeff considered. His reflexes were fast, but he wasn't a fast draw. Worse, his need for answers could make him hesitate.

On the other hand, now that he was sure about Elmer's involvement, he could trace Maggie's journey back along her route and he might still uncover the reason why she had had Cynthia's locket.

'Sure,' he said smiling with ease.

Elmer raised the brim of his hat with one end of the cross, his own smile seeming to acknowledge Jeff's growing confidence.

'Except you have a problem. If you kill Elmer, you won't find out what he knows about Cynthia's fate.'

Jeff's smile grew as Elmer's apparent calm demeanour cracked for the first time.

'That was a mistake, Elmer. Before, I hadn't known there was anything to find out about her, but now I know she's alive and I'll find her.'

That was a guess, but it made Elmer snort a laugh.

He opened his hand and let the cross fall to the ground. Then he withdrew a book from his pocket. When he held it up, Jeff saw that it was a Bible.

The book fell open at a page and Elmer tore that sheet out. Then, while keeping an eye on Jeff, he went down on one knee and rooted through the old fire to find a piece of burnt wood.

With quick gestures he used the charcoal to scrawl two words on the paper. Then he folded the paper and wedged it beneath the cross. With his gaze set on Jeff, he stood and took two backward paces from the cross.

'Die, and die in ignorance,' he said. 'Or live, and read what happened to her.'

'I hope you've provided all the details I'll need.'

'Do you not have faith in Elmer yet?' Elmer settled his stance and drifted his right hand closer to his holster.

'Of course I don't.'

Jeff fixed his gaze on Elmer's blank eyes, hoping to catch the moment when he decided to reach for his gun. In his mind he rehearsed the required motion for his right hand, a quick draw action that he had seldom needed to use before.

Then, with an obvious old trick that he doubted would fool Elmer, he flinched and darted his gaze up past Elmer's left shoulder, as if something had caught his attention.

Elmer didn't look away from him, but Jeff still threw his hand to his holster.

98

His hand hadn't even touched leather when Elmer drew. One moment his hand had been dangling and the next the gun was in his hand, cocked and aimed at him.

For long moments Elmer and Jeff stared at each other. Then, with a roar of defiance and a desperate lunge to the left to confuse Elmer's aim, Jeff grabbed his gun.

Hot fire punched him in the chest, the roar of gunfire and the acrid reek of gunsmoke registering a moment later.

Jeff dropped to his knees where he took a lingering look at the paper that was fluttering in the wind beneath a cross that would now trap its secrets for eternity.

Then he keeled over on to his back and lay looking up at the dark sky that got darker with every heartbeat. He tried to breathe, but only a gasp escaped his lips.

A darker object passed by and he looked up at Elmer, who ran his gaze over his body with a detached air. The sight made Jeff summon his strength. He willed his right arm to rise and shoot him.

To his relief his hand swung up, but it was lighter than he expected and, when he moved the fingers, he found that his gun had fallen from his grasp. Elmer noted his action with a smile before he turned his back on him.

Jeff wheezed a shallow breath, but even that sent a

bolt of pain shooting through his chest. Then Elmer came back holding the slip of paper.

For a moment Jeff thought he'd let him read the message at the last, but instead, he ripped the paper in half and let the pieces go fluttering away.

'Tell me,' Jeff gasped, unable to stop himself from pleading.

'Later,' Elmer said with a smile. Then he turned his back and walked away with a determined tread that said that this time he wouldn't return.

Alone now with just the darkening sky above for company, Jeff closed his eyes. Through a thickening mist he saw a vision of Cynthia, except that now she was older and she was holding out a hand.

Jeff wondered if she wanted her locket back, but she shook her head and beckoned him on.

CHAPTER 10

With one last effort before the strain numbed his arms, Norton dragged his legs up over the edge of the sheer drop. Then, while flexing his aching limbs, he lay on his belly taking calming breaths.

He'd expected never again to enjoy the simple pleasure of lying on solid earth, having spent what felt like an eternity expecting to take a long and final drop down to the ground, probably with a bullet in the back.

But thankfully none of the shots that had been aimed at him had found their target and he'd managed to manoeuvre himself along the edge until he'd found a ledge on which he could place his feet. Then he'd used other ledges and protuberances to draw himself up.

While he rested, he directed his thoughts to wondering what his friends were doing. As they hadn't tried to rescue him, he prepared himself for the worst.

He got to his feet and stepped along the edge of the bluff. Twenty yards on, a ledge came into view. What he saw there confirmed his worst fears. He lowered his head for a moment and then edged closer.

John and Oscar were both lying sprawled with blood pooled around them. Other bodies lay at the bottom of the bluff, but Norton was sure that those men weren't responsible for their deaths.

He swirled round, thinking to go in search of Elmer, but from this position he could see their campsite. Elmer's horse had gone. Strangely, another man was wandering around their camp.

Moving cautiously, he made for the boulder where he'd first spoken with Elmer and then peered around the side. The man was rooting through their belongings. Norton was sure he was one of the men they had helped, so he hailed him. The man flinched, then swung round to face him.

Norton considered the gun in the man's hand calmly.

'Hey,' he said, 'I'm not trouble. I'm Norton Hope. I was with the group that tried to help. . . .'

Norton trailed off when to his surprise he recognized the man as Dewey Shark.

'You were,' Dewey said, 'but last week you were with the group that tried to kill me.'

'I was.' Norton set his hands on his hips. 'But you were stealing everything we had, and I wasn't the one who tried to kill you.'

'I know.' Dewey considered him. 'I guess we can argue about which one of us did the other the most wrong until sunup, but we have a greater problem.'

Dewey's gaze darted to the edge of the bluff and his wide eyes showed more concern about what had happened here than Norton would have expected.

'You mean Elmer Drake?'

'Yeah. He killed your friends over there along with the one we fished out of the river.' Dewey frowned and lowered his tone. 'And now he's moved on, like he always does.'

Norton closed his eyes for a moment and put Elmer from his mind so that he could think about the fate of his friends. He felt only numb now that even the small hope that Albert had got away from Elmer had been extinguished.

'Why are you here?' he spat. The bitterness in his voice made Dewey take a backward step, although he did lower his gun.

'We've been following him for several days. We reckon he has a valuable stolen cross on him.'

Dewey's eagerness made his voice become high-pitched and Norton saw no reason to deny him the information he wanted.

'He has the cross.' Norton smiled when Dewey looked aloft in relief and then holstered his gun. 'Is that what the men who attacked you were looking for?'

Dewey shook his head. 'They had other problems.'

'And where did Elmer go?'

103

Dewey pointed at a crag. 'He went over there and shot up my friend. Then he returned and searched through your belongings. It looked like he stole all your money. Then he collected his horse. I kept down until he'd ridden away. He went east, possibly back along the way we came towards Redemption.'

After seeing how Dewey had behaved in the trading post, Norton reckoned that he had been too scared to confront Elmer, but he kept that thought to himself and turned away.

'Then that's where I'm going.'

Norton moved off, uncaring about what Dewey did next. For his part Dewey watched as Norton gathered his belongings from around the campsite. Dewey said nothing until Norton found a spade.

'We haven't got time to bury the dead,' said Dewey. When Norton scowled, he spread his hands. 'I have friends who died here too, and I know they'd want us to make sure we picked up Elmer's trail tonight while we still have the light.'

Norton considered Dewey's determined stance and, now that he'd made the offer, he had to admit that even though he would never have believed it possible, he'd welcome his help in finding Elmer. The two men nodded to each other and, with that being the extent of the deal they needed to strike, Norton headed to his horse.

A few minutes later, with Dewey walking and Norton leading his horse, they took the long route down the bluff that Norton had climbed up this morning.

When the extent of the carnage that had taken place became visible, Norton stopped. Then as he could think of nothing to say about the scene in front of them, he asked the question that he hadn't asked before.

'Whose cross did Elmer steal?'

Dewey looked downriver to where their quarry would have gone.

'Mine,' he said.

'Anyone there?' Jeff murmured. Then, having heard himself speak, he accepted that he wasn't dead.

He opened his eyes to find that the sky was brighter than it had been when he had thought he was dying. Better still, he was breathing steadily without difficulty.

He raised his hand to bring it into view, also without difficulty, and then placed it on his chest near to where he'd been shot.

Then, with outstretched fingers, he probed tentatively, fearful that he might find out that he was beyond help, after all. He touched frayed cloth and, when he explored the extent of the fraying, a sharp pain thrust through his chest, making him double over and roll on to his side.

This movement intensified the agony and he could do nothing but lie there, hoping it would pass.

By degrees, the pain receded to a dull throb and so, in his doubled-over position he looked down at his chest.

105

The frayed cloth was burnt, so he had been shot and he could see the bullet hole, but there was no blood. Bemused he poked a finger in the hole and the tip jarred against cold metal.

He smiled and then slipped his hand into his breast jacket pocket. He withdrew the silver locket and held it up before his eyes.

A puff of dust rose up from the ruined silver oval that had now been deeply dented. The slug that had caused the damage wasn't embedded in the locket, but with his hopes soaring, he undid his jacket and explored.

Beneath his vest the skin was mottled and sore to the touch suggesting he'd probably cracked a rib, but there was no puncture hole, so he rolled on to his back. While enjoying thinking about the lucky break that had saved his life, he breathed shallowly and dangled the locket on its chain above his face.

As the reflected sunlight dappled across his skin, he accepted that he had survived his showdown with Elmer and that he had been unconscious through the night. Presumably, last night Elmer had thought him dead and so he had moved on.

As nobody had tried to rouse him, Dewey and the last of the prospectors were probably dead too.

Despite this sombre conclusion, he felt elated at the thought that he wouldn't have to deal with his unwelcome partner for any longer. And he'd been left free to track down a man who thought him dead.

Next time, he resolved, he'd avoid a showdown

and just kill Elmer the first chance he got. Then he would seek answers elsewhere.

That thought reminded him about the torn-up sheet of paper and, although he doubted that Elmer had really provided an answer, he searched for it.

The effort of getting to his knees sent another bolt of pain shooting through his chest. It was duller than it had been before, and the discomfort was lessened by the sight of both scraps of paper fluttering amidst the ashes of the old fire.

On hands and knees he crawled to them. The sheets were lying face down, but the dark outline of a single word was visible through each half and so, drawing a long breath, he turned them over.

The word 'beyond' was written on one torn half-page and 'redemption' on the other.

'Beyond redemption,' Jeff said to himself.

He looked aloft while shaking his head. He accepted, without too much disappointment, that Elmer hadn't told him anything about Cynthia's fate. He was about to screw up the two halves when a sudden thought hit him and he stared again at the message.

'You really did tell me the truth about Cynthia,' he said, 'except you didn't expect that I'd understand it.'

Gingerly he clambered to his feet and looked east, back along the route he'd taken to get here, to the distant town of Redemption, a town that a sick Maggie Cartwright, the previous owner of the locket, had left.

There was nothing for most travellers beyond that town, except for the hospital where the sisters of the Sacred Cross cared for the sick and which was run by a nun who believed that no man was beyond redemption.

Jeff smiled as he moved off to confirm the fate of the others.

CHAPTER 11

For several days, the ill-matched duo of Norton Hope and Dewey Shark followed Elmer Drake at a distance.

As they'd expected Elmer retraced his steps to the main river and then along it towards the trading post where Norton had first met him.

The two men rode mainly in silence, Norton being preoccupied with a numbing mixture of anger and sorrow after the deaths of his friends. He presumed Dewey was taken up with thoughts of recovering his stolen cross, along with planning revenge.

As the days passed, the need for revenge also consumed Norton's thoughts, and so, when they were sure that Elmer was heading back to Redemption, Norton tried to discuss plans with Dewey. But Dewey was reluctant to talk and ignored every opportunity to chat.

At first Norton reckoned he didn't trust a man whom he'd assaulted the first time they'd met, but after he'd spent more time with his sullen partner, he decided that Dewey was frightened about the prospect of taking Elmer on.

The only subject Dewey did want to talk about was the lack of liquor. The shakes and cramps that overcame him whenever he realized that he couldn't remedy that situation were enough to put Norton off the thought of drinking when they reached Redemption.

Since Dewey was not sharing his thoughts, Norton developed his own theory that Elmer would look for another group of prospectors to join, and then later kill.

That proved to be incorrect when they found that Elmer had carried on past the trading post and then past Redemption too.

This second discovery annoyed Dewey, as he wanted to head into town and find a saloon. When Norton disagreed, Dewey flinched, as if a matter he had put from his mind had just resurfaced, after which he stopped complaining and they rode on by the town.

With whatever was on Dewey's mind, spurring him on, they speeded up and for the first time they caught a distant sighting of Elmer riding along the railroad tracks towards the entrance to Redemption Gorge. There was nothing beyond that, except the head of the tracks and then the long journey across the Barren Plains.

Norton wasn't welcoming the thought of making that journey, but to his relief Elmer veered away and climbed up a side of the gorge for a short distance. He took up residence looking down at a hospital which, Dewey reported, was run by the nuns of the Sacred Cross.

Norton and Dewey stopped at the entrance to the gorge at a point where Elmer wouldn't be able to see them, then cautiously they made their way closer.

When it became clear that Elmer wasn't doing anything other than watch the building, Dewey pointed out a winding route up the side of the gorge which, he claimed, would keep them hidden from Elmer's view.

Norton didn't question him and Dewey proved he deserved that trust when he led them on to a ledge that was thirty yards higher up than where Elmer was. They both lay on their chests and peered down at him.

'What's he doing?' Dewey whispered after a while.

'He's just sitting there,' Norton said, 'watching the hospital.'

'Or waiting for someone to come out.'

Norton considered the building, wondering if Dewey could be right that Elmer was interested in a patient or perhaps in one of the nuns. Whatever the answer, he doubted that this person would welcome meeting Elmer.

'He's killed too many times already. We can't endanger more people by waiting for him to act. We take him on now.'

Dewey blinked hard, his worried expression

suggesting he'd refuse, but then he gave a reluctant nod. So, using hushed whispers Norton instructed him to sneak up on Elmer from the left while he moved in from the right.

Dewey agreed with this plan and shuffled away. Norton watched him until he disappeared from view. Then he embarked on the roundabout journey that would bring him out on the ledge on which Elmer was sitting.

It took him fifteen minutes, moving slowly and silently, before he reached the right level and faced the tricky problem of coordinating his attack with Dewey. He edged forward to reach a large misshapen boulder. From above, he had seen that he could watch Elmer from there while being safely hidden.

He positioned himself below a low point on the boulder. Then he raised himself slowly to see the ledge.

There were no other places behind which he could take cover between his position and the place where Elmer would be sitting. On Dewey's side, rocks were closer to Elmer's position. Norton looked at them, hoping to catch sight of his partner.

He saw no sign of him, so he raised himself to check on how close Elmer was. Norton winced. Elmer wasn't in the place he'd last seen him and, when he raised himself to a crouched position, he wasn't visible along the length of the ledge.

Norton dropped back down to sit against the boulder where he took stock of the situation.

He'd been careful when getting up to a position above Elmer and again when climbing down. On the other hand Elmer had been sitting still for an hour, so there could be an innocent explanation for his having moved.

Norton stood up and craned his neck. The rocky ledge nearer to him became visible and there was still no sign of Elmer. He raised a leg, intending to clamber up on to the boulder; then he flinched back when Elmer rose up before him.

He just had enough time to register that Elmer must have been lying in wait on the other side of the boulder before Elmer slapped hands on his shoulders. Then Elmer yanked him forward and threw him through the air.

Norton was still too surprised to do anything other than wave his arms before he crashed down on his chest and slid to a halt on the smooth rock.

The blow blasted the air from his lungs and, when he dragged in a breath, he tasted blood. He shook himself, then pushed up with arms that threatened to give way, but he came up to a standing position quickly.

Unfortunately, his jangled senses took a moment to comprehend that he hadn't been responsible for his movement and that Elmer had dragged him up off the ground.

Elmer deposited Norton on his feet, but his legs buckled and he dropped to one knee where he knelt with his head bowed. Without much hope of success, he slipped his hand towards his holster, but the hand closed on air and when he looked up he saw the sheen of gunmetal lying behind Elmer, ten feet away.

This observation gave him renewed hope, as Elmer stared down at him with his head cocked to one side.

'Do you need help in getting up this time?' he asked with an easy smile.

'I didn't need no help the last time,' Norton muttered. 'I don't need it this time.'

'As you wish.' Elmer settled his stance with a slow movement that said he was waiting for Norton's next move and that he was confident it'd fail to harm him.

Norton was still feeling jarred but, mindful of the need to give Dewey enough time to get into position, he pointed at the hospital.

'Why did you come here?'

'Elmer wanted to check that everything was all right.'

'You mean all right with the hospital?' Norton waited for an answer he was sure he wouldn't get. 'Or with someone in it?'

Elmer swung away to look across the gorge. As that movement took his attention away from him, Norton got to his feet. This time he was able to stand without difficulty, but before he could think about confronting Elmer, he saw what had attracted Elmer's interest.

Dewey was scurrying down the side of the gorge and was now just a few paces away from reaching the plains. Norton watched him, wondering how he could have so badly misjudged his attempt to sneak up on Elmer. But Dewey reached flat ground where he thrust his head down and ran on.

With a snarl, Norton accepted the truth that he was abandoning him and saving his own skin.

'Your friend has business elsewhere,' Elmer said.

'That's no friend of mine,' Norton muttered. 'And he won't live for long enough to carry out that business.'

'If you insist. . . .'

Elmer drew his six-shooter and levelled the gun on Dewey's fleeing form. He got a bead on him as he reached the rail tracks in the middle of the gorge.

With a shake of the head, Norton got over his anger and accepted he couldn't let Elmer shoot another man in the back, even if that man was Dewey Shark.

'Don't,' he said and, when Elmer didn't react, he moved down the ledge, intending to go behind Elmer and claim his gun.

Elmer ignored him and fired at Dewey. The gunshot clattered into the rail tracks, sending up a shower of sparks and making Dewey dart from side to side in uncertainty as to which way to run. He chose to head down the centre of the tracks. Grinning Elmer followed his progress with his gun.

Norton reckoned Dewey was probably far enough away to get lucky, so he slipped behind Elmer until he was a few feet from his gun. Then, with hope making his heart beat faster, he reached for the weapon, but Elmer swung round.

He slapped an arm across Norton's chest barring his way. Then he gave a single shake of the head.

Norton looked first at the gun and then at Dewey, who was hightailing it away into the distance. That sight sent a flurry of anger raging in his stomach. He pushed Elmer's arm aside and leaned forward.

Elmer slapped a heavy hand down on Norton's back and held him steady. Then he dragged him up to an upright position and swung him round.

The two men glared at each other until, with a casual move, Elmer raised Norton off the ground and hurled him aside. Norton could do nothing to avoid slamming backwards into the rock face behind him.

He stood propped up against the solid rock. His battered body felt as if it was a bug that had been crushed beneath a boot.

Then he tried to take a step forward, but the effort only succeeded in making him slide down the rock on to his rump, where he looked up at the advancing Elmer.

A firm hand was wrapped around his vest front and he was again bodily lifted off the ground. Elmer drew him up to look at him eye to eye.

Norton struggled to free himself, but Elmer held him securely and, worse, his tight grip squeezed Norton's windpipe. He could drag in only a wheez-

116

ing gasp of air before that too was cut off. With darkness clawing at the edges of his vision, Norton looked
down.

Then, taking careful aim, he launched a scything
kick at Elmer's kneecap. The toe of his boot
crunched into its target and, although he couldn't
put much force behind the blow, it still made Elmer
grunt in pain and stumble.

The tight grip around Norton's neck relaxed and
he breathed in a grateful mouthful of cool air. But in
his weak state that was all he could do and he
dropped down to the ground where the two men
swayed before they both fell over.

They hit the hard ledge on their sides with their
limbs entangled. Then, with a disorientating movement, they both rolled over and dropped.

Through his befuddled senses, the realization
dawned on Norton that they had fallen off the end of
the ledge, but by then it was too late to still his
motion.

Norton, along with Elmer, went rolling down the
rocky slope. With a series of jarring thuds and scraping slides, Norton fell and he could do nothing to
stop his painful progress.

A scream rent the air and Norton was too busy
trying to grab hold of something to know if he had
made the noise.

For a seeming eternity the sky and ground swirled
around him. He felt that he must have collided with
every rock on the way down until, with a nauseating

thud, Norton came to rest lying on his back.

He forced himself to move and the best he could manage in his battered state was to lever himself up to a sitting position. Aching muscles and grating bones accompanied every movement, but he put the injuries from his mind when he saw that Elmer was lying beside him on his chest.

Norton searched for Elmer's gun, but he couldn't see it. He looked for another weapon. A rock that was about two feet in diameter was near by.

He limped to the rock, over which he stood hunched and swaying. The ground appeared to be coming up to meet him and he didn't think he could remain conscious for long. So quickly he put both hands to the rock.

Shouting from the effort, he raised the heavy rock to waist height, which he reckoned was high enough for him to dash it down fatally on Elmer's head. But the effort of supporting the rock made him feel light-headed.

After taking a single pace towards Elmer, he fell sideways and crashed to the ground.

The rock thudded down to earth ineffectually several feet from Elmer's head, after which Norton struggled to keep his eyes open.

He must have passed out as the next he knew people were talking near by. Then a woman's face glared down at him with wide and irritated eyes.

'I'm Sister Angelica,' she said. 'I help the sick and injured. That includes you.'

118

Norton tried to answer, but sleep felt more inviting. He surrendered to the dark.

CHAPTER 12

'And how may the nuns of the Sacred Cross serve you this time?' Sister Angelica said, using her usual stern tone that made Jeff pleased that he was no longer in pain and so needful of that help.

Jeff offered the nun a smile that only served to deepen her frown.

'I heard that two men needing your help were brought in here yesterday.'

'That's correct.' She took a short pace forward to block the door to the hospital and folded her arms.

'Then,' Jeff said when it became clear that she wouldn't volunteer any further information, 'I'd be obliged if I could see them.'

'You may not.'

She took a step backwards and moved to slam the door, forcing Jeff to jerk forward to try to slip in through the closing gap. This only encouraged her to close the door more forcefully, trapping an arm and a leg.

'It'd be easier for us all if you just let me see my friends,' Jeff grunted, as he tried and failed to lever the door open while not putting pressure on his weak ribs.

She pressed on the door all the harder, pinning him in place. After he had endured a painful impasse for thirty seconds, she released the door. So, with a grateful sigh, Jeff moved forward, but she had only been giving him room to leave and, as he'd moved forward instead of backwards, she hammered her full weight against the door.

This time the edge of the door dug into Jeff's ribs. He screeched in pain. Then he kicked and shoved until he managed to squeeze his body out of the doorway after which she slammed the door to. Outside, he leaned back against the wall taking shallow breaths while holding his ribs.

The pain was subsiding when the door opened a fraction and Angelica peered out.

'Are you hurt?' she said.

'Will you slam the door in my face again if I say no?'

'I will.' She considered the hand he'd pressed to his side and then his tight-jawed expression. 'You may come in and I'll tend to the injury you've inflicted upon yourself. But only if you hand over your gun.'

'Obliged,' Jeff said while tentatively taking a step inside, but on the second step Angelica slapped a hand down on his arm.

'But if you distress my other patients, I'll add to your pain.'

'I don't doubt it.' Jeff laughed, but when Angelica only glared at him, he moved on to the room that she indicated.

This room turned out to be on the opposite side to the annexe where he'd spent the night last week. It had a roof and it was sparsely furnished with a table, chair and cupboard. There was another door in the room beyond which he heard low muttering that suggested other more badly injured people were being cared for.

Angelica positioned herself between him and the door in a way that suggested he'd been correct. But he didn't act on that knowledge. Instead, he removed his gun and holster and laid it on the table beside two large plates. Then he let her see the wound, which now had a diffused yellow and red mottling.

While she bound his chest, he ventured several offhand comments hoping to engage her in conversation that he could direct towards discovering whether what he'd surmised was correct. But she wasn't the type for conversation and she passed up every opportunity with ease.

This morning Jeff had ridden into Redemption after following Elmer as well as two survivors of the gun battle. He had asked for information in the saloon in which he'd met Dewey Shark. He'd figured that men who avoided the law congregated here. He

122

would be safe from reprisals from the surviving posse members, if they had made their way back.

He'd been told a story that two men had attacked another man, presumably Elmer, near to the hospital. Two men had been hurt while one man had fled the scene.

Jeff assumed that the man who had got away was Elmer leaving Dewey and the surviving prospector in need of the sisters' help. There was no news of Marshal Root's posse and he was surprised that Dewey had resisted the urge to come to town for liquor, but Jeff hadn't waited around to confirm the details.

'Does that feel better?' Angelica said, stepping back to consider her work.

Jeff flexed his chest against the tight bandages, finding that although they restricted his movements his chest was less painful.

'It does,' he said with a smile that he didn't need to force. He shrugged back into his clothes. 'How can I repay someone who is here to serve without asking for anything in return?'

'By praying and doing good,' she snapped, her narrowed eyes showing she'd noted his sarcasm. 'Money also helps.'

Jeff dug in his pocket. He counted out a dollar on to the plate that she presented to him. Then, through force of habit, he moved to provide more. But before he could add anything to the dollar on the plate he drew his hand back.

'I'd like to talk with my friends,' he said, looking at the money in his hand.

She considered the money and then gave a brief nod.

'You have two minutes.' She took all the money from his hand and deposited it on the plate.

'Obliged for—'

'And that time has already started.'

Jeff wasted no time in hurrying on to the door with Angelica at his shoulder. The other room turned out to be as he'd imagined it, with beds laid out on both sides.

Two beds were occupied. Another nun, whom he took to be Sister Verena from her build, had her back to him. She was changing the dressing on a patient's forehead. When Jeff had taken a few steps into the room, he confirmed that the man wasn't Dewey.

He moved on down the aisle. This let him see beyond the nun to the patient in the corner. He saw a man, larger than the first. A wet towel covered his face, but Jeff was sure he wasn't Dewey either.

The worrying thought hit Jeff that if two people had been injured in the altercation, it didn't follow that Elmer was the one who had escaped injury.

'Are these men your friends?' Angelica asked in a sceptical tone as he edged closer.

'I'm not sure,' Jeff said. 'I could have been wrong.'

He moved back to stand at the foot of the first bed, where he watched Verena clean a nasty scrape on the patient's forehead. He considered him and judged

124

that he had the same stature as the man he'd seen dangling over the edge of a sheer drop in the Redemption Mountains.

On the other hand he'd been some distance away and many men were the same size as he was.

The second man presented the same problem: that, although he was of the same build as Elmer, he didn't have to be him. He moved forward meaning to remove the towel from his face, but Angelica perceived his intention. She stepped in front of him.

'This is Mark,' she said. 'The other man hasn't stayed conscious for long enough yet to provide a name.'

'I'd heard they were fighting. Is it wise to keep them together?'

Angelica bristled and Verena tensed, presumably in anticipation of the tirade to come.

'It's not wise for a man who's using up his last minute to question my orders,' Angelica said. 'The nuns of the Sacred Cross treat all men the same, but, since you asked, Mark is a gentle man and this other man is too injured to do him harm.'

She set her hands on her hips defying Jeff to disagree. When he said nothing she turned away, removed the towel from Mark's face, and placed it in a bowl of water.

The man's dark eyes were already open and he was looking up at the roof.

'That's not Mark,' Jeff snapped. 'That's Elmer.'

The patient's only reaction was to close his eyes.

Angelica placed the towel back over his brow.

'You're mistaken,' she said, 'and your time is now over. I hope seeing your friends gave you solace.'

'It didn't. That man's a killer.'

'He's a man who's in need of our care, again.' Angelica bustled round the bed and shooed him away. 'And you're in the way.'

Jeff stood his ground, but not for long when confronted by the unstoppable force that was Sister Angelica. She barged into him, thankfully avoiding his bruised ribs, and then shepherded him away. Verena accompanied them towards the door and, by the time Jeff had wrestled himself free of Angelica, he was back in the smaller room.

'Rest assured,' Jeff said, picking up his gun, 'I'll have to use this if you don't let me take that man away while he's still too hurt to defend himself.'

Angelica considered the gun with contempt and drew out a plain wooden cross from around her neck.

'This is all the protection I need.' She stared at him and, when Jeff sneered, she lowered her head to remove the cross and slapped it into his hand. 'And you'll be better served to trust this instead of your gun.'

Jeff waved the cross at her. 'This won't help none against a man who has no qualms about killing men, women, children.'

'I've heard of such men, but Mark isn't one of them. He once helped here and now he's returned.'

126

Jeff tapped the cross against his other palm as he pieced together what he thought he knew about the situation.

'Six months ago you found him lying half-dead after he'd been hanged and dragged along by the neck. You knew he must have done wrong, but you reckoned that no man was beyond redemption and so you nursed him back to health.'

'You're right. I gave him a second chance, which he has taken.' Angelica pointed at the door with a stern finger. 'Now go!'

Jeff ignored the finger and fixed her with his gaze.

'He lay low here for a while licking his wounds, but after he left, he went back to the old ways that got him half-killed in the first place.'

'The man you describe isn't Mark.'

'I know. I'm describing Elmer Drake and—'

The hitherto silent Verena uttered a strangulated screech, making Angelica swirl round to face her. Jeff hadn't seen this woman's features properly before, but now she was looking at him. She'd put a hand over her mouth to silence her outburst and a cowl covered her head, but her eyes were visible and they were familiar.

They were the eyes of a young woman, a woman he'd last seen when she was a child.

'Cynthia?' Jeff murmured.

127

CHAPTER 13

'You're wrong,' Angelica said. 'This is Sister Verena.'

'She isn't,' Jeff said as the silent nun lowered her gaze. 'She's a young woman whom everyone presumed to have died ten years ago.'

Angelica shook her head. 'Last month Verena gave herself to our order, and you've already taken up far too much of her and my time.'

Jeff ignored Angelica and continued to look at Verena – if that was what she wished to call herself, waiting for her to speak. Verena furrowed her brow and, the situation clearly distressing her, she opened and closed her mouth several times before she spoke.

'I'm Sister Verena,' she said, her voice catching with a sob which made Angelica nod and then swirl round to face Jeff with a triumphant gleam in her eye.

'There's your answer,' Angelica said. 'Now go.'

'I know you're good people, but I need ... I

deserve a better answer than that. A whole town thought Cynthia Harris had died and now here stands a grown woman who looks like what I reckon that fourteen-year-old girl would look like now.'

Angelica ushered him to the door, but Jeff shook off the hand and moved forward to stand before the nun. He removed the damaged locket from his pocket and held it high.

Verena watched the locket swing gently from side to side. Then, with a sigh, she looked him in the eye.

'Why do you have that?'

'I got it from Maggie Cartwright,' Jeff said, choosing a suitable answer. Then he hazarded a guess. 'She was sick and you looked after her. Before you gave yourself to the order, you gave this to her to rid yourself of everything that reminded you of your past life.'

Verena gulped and glanced at Angelica before she replied.

'The girl who owned that locket before Maggie,' she said in a matter-of-fact manner as if reading aloud, 'had a terrible life. She saw her family lying dead and she was taken from her home. Alone and blindfolded, she escaped on to the streets of Beaver Ridge, where her life became even worse. But with the kindness of others she found peace. She never saw the man who killed her family, but even if she had, a woman who tends to those in need would bear no malice.'

While Angelica glowered at him, Jeff ran that

statement through his mind, wondering whether it had confirmed that Verena was the girl he had known as Cynthia. He decided it did. He offered her a smile that made her eyes narrow briefly, suggesting she wanted to return it but knew she couldn't.

'Why Verena?' he asked.

She turned away quickly, as if she'd already said too much, and busied herself with tidying away the rest of the bandage roll that Angelica had used to bind his chest.

'Verena was a nurse who cared for the sick,' Angelica said. She stared at the nun's back with her expression stern, confirming that Verena had overstepped the boundaries within which she now lived her life. 'That's a good choice of name for a sister of the Sacred Cross.'

Jeff nodded, but the solving of one problem only focused his mind on his other problem.

'I have to deal with the man in there,' he said. 'No matter what he's calling himself now, he's evil.'

'He does good work.' Angelica went to the table and removed a rag that had been draped over a second plate. Underneath was money and the jewelled cross. 'He took the cross for comfort and now he's returned it along with an impressive donation. We'll now be able to complete the work on the hospital.'

'I doubt he got that money honestly. Three prospectors are lying dead up in the mountains and then there's Maggie. She never reached her destination.

She's dead.'

Verena squealed. Angelica grabbed his arm and marched him to the door and then down the corridor to the main door.

'Your injuries have been tended,' she said, opening the door. 'And we have work to do.'

'I'll return at the first sign of trouble,' Jeff said. When Angelica closed the door, he stuck a boot in the way, halting it and looked past her at Verena, who had come out into the corridor. 'And whatever happens, I'll make sure the people who cared about Cynthia know what happened to her.'

'That would please Cynthia,' Verena said with a catch in her throat.

Jeff's heart thudded with a concern that he couldn't identify. To cover his confusion he looped the locket back into his hand. Angelica then pushed the door and this time her shove sent him stumbling outside.

As the door slammed shut, he stared at the ground, wondering why Cynthia's . . . *Verena's*, as he now had to think of her, parting comment had worried him.

Then he identified his concern. She had spoken about herself in the same impersonal way that Elmer had spoken about himself.

In expectation that he'd almost understood Elmer's motivation, he rummaged in his pocket and removed the page from the Bible on which Elmer had written the cryptic message that had led him here. The page had a heading that identified it as being from the Gospel of Mark.

'Like the nuns, you adopted the name of someone you revered,' he said to himself, 'but why such a good man?'

He stared at the closed door until he noticed that lying before him was the plain cross that he must have dropped while being rudely shoved outside. With a smile, he remembered Angelica's last words.

He gathered up the cross. Then, with it resting on a palm, he walked away from the building at a confident pace. He even managed a tuneless whistle for the benefit of anyone who might be close enough to hear.

When he reached his horse he examined the cross from various angles, seeking the best light, while also ensuring that it could be seen from both sides of the gorge. He tossed it in the air, juggled with it, and even punched the air in triumph.

Then he led his horse over to the opposite side of the gorge to the place where he'd been told the fight had taken place. He clambered up the side for a few dozen yards until he found a ledge where he could rest in full sunlight.

He placed the wooden cross at his side and then, with half of his attention on the hospital, he waited.

He didn't have to wait for long before he had the feeling that he was being watched. Shortly after that he heard grit scraping to his side. He picked up the cross and transferred it to his pocket, the action both hiding its worthless nature from scrutiny and his drawing of his gun.

He waited until he heard grit move again. Then he aimed the gun towards the sound.

'Come out, Dewey,' he said with a weary air.

A gasp sounded from someone out of Jeff's view.

'I'm staying right here,' Dewey called.

'Quit worrying. I don't blame you for running away from Elmer Drake.' Jeff waited and a few moments later Dewey emerged from behind a rock with his gun drawn but held low. 'Although I do blame you for leaving me for dead.'

Dewey halted. 'Hey, I really did think Elmer had killed you. So I went looking for that cross that had excited Wilfred, but it seems you got your hands on it first.'

'I did. Are you ready to negotiate now?'

'You'll really give me the cross?' Dewey asked, edging forward.

'I only want Elmer and he's lying injured on a hospital bed alongside one of the prospectors.'

'That's Norton Hope. The two of us joined forces to take on Elmer. We failed.'

Dewey sat beside him sporting a shamefaced look that suggested he was unwilling to relate the full tale. From the corner of his eye Dewey looked around on the ground, presumably for the cross.

'Are you willing to try again?' Jeff asked.

'Sure. But give me the cross first.' Dewey shrugged when Jeff uttered a rueful laugh. 'You can trust me to

133

cover your back again like I did in the mountains.'

Dewey's wide grin didn't convince Jeff of his honesty. It removed his last shred of concern about playing a cruel trick on the only man who might help him.

'You did help me back there, so perhaps you should get what you deserve.' Jeff reached into his pocket, making Dewey lean forward. 'But put your gun down on the ledge first. I want no tricks.'

Dewey did as ordered and then held out a hand. Slowly, Jeff removed the cross from his pocket. Then, before Dewey could see that it was only wooden, he tossed it away.

Dewey followed the cross's progress. It even caught a beam of sunlight and shone, giving credence to Jeff's subterfuge for a few more seconds. Then the cross crashed down on the ledge and broke into two halves.

Dewey hurried over to the remnants of the cross and stood over them. Then he kicked them aside and swirled round to face Jeff.

'It's a worthless lump of wood,' he snapped. He set his hands on his hips. 'Why the lie?'

'That's a mighty fine question.' Jeff raised his gun making Dewey thrust up his hands, but he stilled the motion with the gun aimed at Dewey's left foot. 'Are you sure you want the answer?'

Dewey sighed. 'I'll tell you the truth. No matter what you threaten me with, I'm not helping you take on Elmer.'

'That's the right answer.'

Jeff waited until Dewey smiled hopefully. Then he fired. Loud gunfire sounded closely followed by Dewey's even louder screech of pain as he jumped up and down on one leg.

'You shot off my foot,' he screamed. He stopped jumping to glare at the red hole in his boot that promised he had at worst lost only a toe.

'That looks sore,' Jeff said, appraising the hole. 'I reckon I need to take you to the hospital and get it fixed up.'

A nun was standing over his bed and looking down at him. As it wasn't the stern Angelica, Norton smiled.

'Am I going to be all right?' he said, his voice emerging as a croak as he tried to get up.

'Don't ask questions,' the nun urged. 'They'll only distress you.'

Norton reckoned that that was good advice and he lay down on his back. While looking up at the roof, he listened to the nun checking on the other patients, but the moment he heard her leave, he took stock of his situation.

He was lying in a hospital bed. When he raised his head, he saw that in the bed beside him was the man he had tried to kill, but now Elmer was lying peacefully with his hands on his chest looking up.

As Elmer appeared as weak and as unthreatening as he himself felt, he craned his neck to see who else was in the hospital. Only one other patient was in the room, but to Norton's irritation that man was Dewey.

He was sitting up in the bed opposite and he was staring at Elmer with wide-open eyes. Even the sight of Norton stirring didn't diminish his terror.

'I didn't run away,' Dewey said without conviction. 'I was trying to get close to Elmer from a different direction.'

'Every bone in my body aches,' Norton said, 'and I feel like I fell down the side of a mountain, which is just about what I did do. I haven't got the strength to argue with you.'

'I got hurt too.' Dewey raised a heavily bandaged foot and pointed at it. 'That proves I wasn't scared of him.'

Norton couldn't remember everything that had happened during his fight with Elmer, but he doubted Dewey had been injured during the incident. He still shrugged.

'All that matters is that the three of us have been left in here alone. I can barely raise my head, but a man with only a sore foot who isn't scared of Elmer can end this now.'

'This isn't my battle no more,' Dewey murmured. 'I'm finding the proper cross and then I'm getting out of here.'

With that resolution, Dewey sat up on the side of the bed. With his bandaged foot raised high, he hopped to the wall where he stood on one leg, watching the comatose Elmer.

'I don't know for sure that Elmer has it now,'

Norton said.

Dewey sighed. 'I guess there's only one way to find out.'

Dewey took a deep breath and then embarked on the short trip to the side of Elmer's bed. He looked him over. Then, with outstretched fingers, as if he were too worried even to touch him, he patted Elmer's pockets. He searched through two without success, then moved on to the breast pocket.

His fingers were just slipping into the pocket when, with a sudden movement, Elmer slapped a hand down on his wrist making him screech. Elmer's head jerked down to transfix Dewey with his dark gaze.

'That wasn't the right way,' Elmer said. Then he thrust his arm up high and threw Dewey away from him.

Dewey couldn't support himself and he slammed into the wall, rebounded, and then went tumbling. From the floor he peered up at Elmer, but Elmer had already turned his attention to Norton.

With no sign of discomfort Elmer swung his legs off the bed and got to his feet. He loomed over Norton, who tried to move off his bed, but he was as weak as he feared he'd be and he only rocked ineffectually from side to side.

Elmer slapped two hands down on his shoulders and then knelt on the bed to look down at him. Norton put his hands to Elmer's forearms and tried to shove them away, but the arms were like stone and

137

he couldn't stop Elmer moving his hands in to grip his neck.

Looking past Elmer's side, he saw Dewey get up, stand on one foot and hop in uncertain paces towards the bed.

'Help me, Dewey,' Norton said, without any hope that he'd now overcome his fear of Elmer, 'before he kills us all.'

'You got that right,' Elmer whispered as he pressed his fingers in. 'Now, tell me: do you have faith in me?'

'I don't,' Norton gasped, surprised by the question despite the situation. 'But you didn't call yourself Elmer.'

'That's because I lost faith in myself for a while.' Elmer widened his eyes. 'Now I have it back.'

Then he tightened his hands.

CHAPTER 14

The sun had disappeared below the top of the gorge when Dewey came out of the hospital. He didn't give the prearranged signal; instead he hobbled off down the gorge.

Jeff was too disgusted by his behaviour to go after him, and so he headed across the tracks to the hospital. He presumed that Dewey hadn't confronted Elmer, but it was likely that his presence had raised consternation. So he resolved that this time he wouldn't heed Angelica's concerns. However, before he'd reached the door, Dewey stopped his fitful progress towards the entrance to the gorge.

He shuffled round on the spot and then made his slow way back, but Jeff soon saw that he hadn't reconsidered. Four riders were heading towards him and they were spreading out as they sought to round him up.

Worse, Deputy Eddie Bell was leading the group. When he saw Jeff further up the gorge, Bell ignored

Dewey and galloped on towards him.

Jeff hurried to the door and pushed. It didn't move, so he hammered on it. He didn't call for Angelica, figuring that if she heard his voice it was less likely that she would open the door.

'Stay there and you'll live,' Bell called.

Jeff knocked on the door one more time, but when he heard nothing beyond, he turned and spread his hands.

'Don't waste time arresting me,' he shouted as Bell dismounted. 'The nuns are in danger.'

'Thinking of others again, are we?' Bell said in a sarcastic tone. 'Just like you did when you helped Dewey escape justice and just like—'

'We can argue about this later,' Jeff snapped. 'All that matters is that you arrest a man in there before it's too late.'

Bell glanced down the gorge at Dewey, who had given up trying to escape and was now sitting on the ground examining his foot with more concern than he was giving to the circling riders. Then Bell considered Jeff. For long moments his steady gaze made Jeff think he'd relent, but then Bell shook his head.

'I decide whom I arrest, and I'm starting with you.' He gestured at Dewey. 'Join your accomplice and then my fellow deputies will take you back to town.'

'People will die because of you,' Jeff snapped. Again he slammed a heavy fist on the door.

It returned only a hollow thud, but he consoled himself with the thought that as he couldn't hear anything happening inside, it was possible that Elmer was still incapacitated.

When he turned back, Bell had advanced on him with his gun aimed at his chest. Seeing no other choice Jeff handed over his gun. With his hands raised, he moved on to join Dewey.

They had yet to reach Dewey when Jeff heard the door creak open. He halted, making Bell walk into him before he pushed him on, but Jeff stuck out a foot and then swirled round. To his surprise, Verena had come out.

'Wait,' she called. 'Angelica got it wrong. Elmer's attacking one of our patients.'

Jeff moved to push Bell aside, but the deputy reacted quickly and grabbed his arm. Then, using an efficient action that Jeff had often used himself to secure prisoners, Bell twisted Jeff's arm and swung him round to hold him with the arm thrust up his back.

'Last chance to get only arrested,' Bell muttered in his ear. When Jeff gave a brief nod, Bell looked at Verena. 'Who's Elmer?'

'Elmer Drake,' she said with a gulp, seemingly only then noticing that she'd used his real name. 'He's been calling himself Mark, but—'

'Save the explanations for later.'

Bell gestured with his free hand for the other deputies to bring Dewey forward. Then he gave them brief orders to go into the hospital and apprehend Elmer.

141

Without catching Jeff's eye, Dewey sat down and joined them in watching the deputies head inside.

'Obliged you've acted,' Jeff said, 'but I can help. And believe me, you'll need help to arrest Elmer.'

While Bell tightened his grip, Dewey snorted and then shuffled round to look away from the hospital. He stood and prodded a spreading red patch on his bandaged foot. Verena also tore her gaze away from the building. After catching Bell's eye and receiving a nod, she knelt down beside Dewey and examined his foot.

'Your help hasn't made anything better,' Bell said.

Jeff couldn't argue with that assessment. He watched Verena encourage Dewey to hold out his foot while showing him more compassion than he deserved.

'Admitting that Angelica was wrong took courage, Sister Verena,' Jeff said to stop him dwelling on what could be happening inside. 'And it took even more courage to cope with knowing that Elmer's in there.'

'I knew from the injuries he'd suffered before Angelica found him that he'd probably done questionable things,' she said while unwinding Dewey's bandage. 'But Angelica had already told me to forgive Elmer . . . Mark, so discovering who he was and that his activities had personally affected me changed nothing.'

Jeff had heard her speak often enough now to know that she had struggled to make that declaration and that she was saying the words Angelica wanted her to say. As Dewey was flashing Jeff a sly look that acknowledged his role in inflicting those injuries, he didn't press her.

'Why did he call himself Mark?'

'That was Angelica's doing. While nursing him, she told him he would recover and be a better man. She spoke of Saint Mark.' She looked up from her work with her expression tense. 'He was killed by being dragged through the streets by his neck.'

Dewey jerked his foot away from Verena while muttering an oath that made her flinch. Bell gestured at him.

'Keep that mouth closed,' he said, 'or—'

He broke off when a gunshot sounded inside the hospital closely followed by two more. The commotion made Dewey attempt to gain his feet. Bell moved towards him.

His movement made him loosen the grip he had around Jeff's arm. Jeff braced his back and tore himself free. The action made both men stumble, but Jeff used the momentum to break into a run towards the hospital. Both Verena and Bell shouted at him to stop, but Jeff kept going.

With every pace he expected a bullet in the back, but he reached the door unharmed. He looked back to see that the others hadn't followed him. Bell was standing over Dewey while Verena was remonstrating with them both.

Jeff put them from his mind and hurried inside, where he found that after the gunfire all was silent.

143

He figured that if Elmer had been arrested there would be animated sounds of activity. Cautiously, he made his way to the annexe where Elmer had been lying.

When he opened the door leading into the small room where he'd been tended, he saw the first sign of trouble.

One of the deputies was lying in the middle of the room on his back. His chest was holed; the same fate had been suffered by a second man, who lay in the doorway to the main room, his body keeping the door propped open.

From beyond the door a low and pitiful sobbing was sounding.

'Don't,' a man murmured.

A gunshot sounded, closely followed by the thud of a body hitting the floor. Jeff moved on to the nearest body. He wrested the gun from the dead man's hand, then stood beside the door. He reckoned that for a brief moment when Elmer emerged he wouldn't be visible.

He waited, but all was silent. When a door creaked it was the one leading to the corridor. Angelica appeared. She held on to the door with one hand while she pressed the other to a livid bruise on her forehead.

'He turned on you too?' Jeff said.

Angelica ignored him and considered the bodies on the floor. Then she set her gaze on the next door and embarked on the journey across the room.

Her steps were faltering and on the third pace she started to fall. Jeff grabbed her before she could drop, then moved her round to prop her up against the wall.

'Mark still in there?' she said, her voice the weakest he had ever heard it.

'*Elmer* will come out soon,' Jeff said, 'and people are waiting for him.'

'No more bloodshed. I'll deal with him.'

She attempted to push him away, but the effort was weak and she slumped back against the wall.

'Stay here. If he comes out, talk with him.'

He looked at her until she nodded. Then he turned to the door, but her gaze took in the gun he now held and she grabbed his arm. He tried to wrest himself free without injuring her, but she held on resolutely.

Their scuffing echoed in the room. He slapped a hand over her mouth and conveyed with a pained expression the need for silence.

She continued to struggle and her movements sent the cross around her neck jerking around. It was the jewelled one and he was surprised that Elmer hadn't taken it, but then, Elmer had never been motivated by the need for money, only the need to kill.

That thought made Jeff look at the simple rope that she wore as a belt. With a smile he removed his hand from her mouth and undid the rope.

'What are you doing?' she screeched as the rope

dropped away and her habit opened, forcing her to release him.

He averted his eyes while tying a quick knot, then fashioning the rope into a noose. He moved to the side of the door.

'Hey, Elmer,' he called. 'Here's a present from Dewey, something that's already defeated you.'

He tossed the noose through the door where it landed ten feet away and neatly splayed out, with the noose end facing the door and the other end trailing down the aisle between the beds.

'But it didn't,' Elmer said, his voice coming from the far end of the room. 'There was a time when that would have worried me and made me question myself, but not now. I came back from the dead and now I'm as strong as I ever was.'

Jeff heard that his way of speaking had changed.

'And so did I. You shot me and yet I've returned.'

Elmer laughed. 'I wonder if you can do it for a second time.'

'I was thinking the same about you.'

Jeff waited for Elmer to continue with the taunting, but his nemesis stayed silent. So he rehearsed in his mind the motion of leaping in through the doorway and shooting Elmer.

Bearing in mind the ease with which Elmer had won their first showdown, he doubted that he could accomplish the task and, as the door wasn't hinged on his side, the necessary manoeuvre he required would be even harder.

With a quick change of mind, he took a deep breath and jumped forward.

CHAPTER 15

Jeff leapt over the body lying in the doorway to reach the other side of the door as, inside the room, a gunshot cracked and then cannoned through the doorway into the corner.

Elmer had reacted quickly, but not quickly enough. He'd also shown Jeff that he'd moved to the opposite wall.

Jeff glanced at Angelica, who was clutching her cross while offering a silent prayer. Jeff reckoned he'd need that prayer and, with one of his own on his lips, he leapt through the doorway.

He went in low and threw himself to the floor. His quick motion saved him from a second shot that scythed over his back. Then he slid across the polished floor on his chest and fetched up behind a bed.

His ribs protested and he was sure something in his chest gave way, but he was more relieved to have got inside unscathed. Gritting his teeth against the pain, he put a hand to the underside of the bed.

Then he stood up.

Thankfully, the bed tipped over and he ended up standing with the bed held before him as a shield. The bedding fell away to reveal wooden slats. They were thick, but they wouldn't withstand an onslaught for long.

Jeff thrust a hand around the side of the bed and fired blind. A sharp pain in the wrist made him open the hand. A moment later he registered that Elmer had shot at his gun and had knocked it from his grip.

As the weapon clattered to the floor and then skittered along to lie beside the noose, Jeff jerked his hand back, then moved on to the wall.

'I can see you through the gaps,' Elmer said with delight. 'You're even less fun to kill than the others were.'

Jeff moved his head so that he could see Elmer between two slats. He was standing six feet away with his leading foot resting beside the end of the rope. The body of the third deputy lay draped over a bed, but that was the only body Jeff could see.

Jeff reckoned Norton should be in here. When he ran his gaze over the room again, he saw him.

Norton was sitting on the floor between two beds. He was propped up against the wall with his head bowed. Then, almost as if he'd realized he was being watched, he raised his head.

The movement was jerky and, when Jeff saw his face, it was contorted with pain, but the man was still alive.

149

'Killing isn't fun,' Jeff said, saying anything to keep Elmer talking for a few more moments.

'It is if you do it right.' Elmer kicked the rope. 'And Dewey didn't know nothing.'

'That's the only thing you've said that I do understand,' Jeff blurted out.

He watched Norton walk his hand up the wall to the table that stood beside the bed. He thought he was aiming to drag himself up to his feet, but instead he grabbed the oil lamp.

Only two lit lamps were in the gloomy room. The light-level flickered, sending shadows scooting around the room, but Elmer didn't register that he'd noticed. Instead, his gaze turned to the door.

Jeff looked over his shoulder to see that Sister Angelica had made her way as far as the doorway. She still clutched her cross as if she really believed it was the only protection she needed.

'Stay back,' Elmer said. 'I owe you my life, but I've already repaid that debt.'

'Giving me money didn't repay your debt,' Angelica said. She took another pace to reveal that in her other hand she held the plate which held the money Elmer had given her. She tipped the plate up to spill the bills on the floor. 'Changing your life would have.'

'I considered it,' Elmer said. 'I didn't like the thought.'

'I had faith that you would.' Angelica took another pace forward. 'I still have faith that you can.'

'Nah,' Elmer said with ease. Then he raised his gun, moving it slowly towards Jeff as he savoured the act.

Jeff stayed his hand until the last moment, when he planned to throw the bed at Elmer, but through the slats he saw Norton raise the lamp.

Then, with his other hand clutching his stomach, Norton launched the lamp at Elmer. The effort jerked him forward while the lamp skewed feet wide of its target and landed on a bed, splashing burning oil in all directions.

With a whoosh the bedding burst into flame making Elmer swirl round to face Norton.

Elmer slammed a shot into Norton's chest that made him slide sideways to lie in a crumpled heap. Norton didn't make a sound, as if the effort of throwing the lamp had taken his last ounce of strength.

Before Elmer could turn back, Jeff raised the bed off the floor and hurled it at him.

Elmer reacted quickly, but while his gun was still swinging round towards Jeff, the bed collided with his arm and jerked it aside. Jeff threw himself at his own gun.

He slid across the floor and got tangled up with the rope, forcing him to waste valuable moments freeing himself. Then he rolled behind the burning bed. When he stopped moving, he was holding the gun.

He pressed his left hand to his aching chest and then leapt to his feet, his gun swinging up with a swift motion that stilled when he found that Elmer had got his wits about him. The bed lay on its side and Elmer stood before it.

Through the rising flames the two men considered each other. Jeff's gun was aimed at the floor. Elmer's gun was already aimed at his chest. With his hand on his wounded chest, Jeff felt the locket in his pocket.

'It's later,' Jeff said. He withdrew the locket and let it hang from a finger. 'It's time to tell me why you didn't kill the girl.'

'That locket looks shot up,' Elmer said. 'It's almost as if someone with quick reflexes and perfect aim deliberately shot at it.'

Jeff couldn't avoid wincing, having not considered that possibility.

'It is, and maybe you did spare my life, but why? Did you need the truth about her to come out so that Angelica, or perhaps even Verena herself, would know you'd once done a good act? Or did you need others to have faith in you before you could have it in yourself?'

Elmer shrugged. 'Maybe I find it too easy sometimes and not enough fun.'

'You know that's not right,' Angelica said. 'You can do good, and you have done it. Hanging from Jeff's finger is the proof that once you stilled your hand when you could have killed.'

Elmer snarled and swung the gun away from Jeff to aim it at her.

'I didn't. I planned to kill her later!'

The flames were now licking at blankets that had been stacked up on a cupboard by the wall. Within moments they spread to the bed behind Jeff, making him feel as though he was being roasted from all sides.

'Whatever the truth,' Angelica said, 'you're not beyond redemption.'

Elmer dropped to one knee briefly and grabbed the rope. When he stood up, he let the rope swing from his free hand. A stray splash of burning oil had landed on the rope and flames were scooting round the noose.

'But I am. I can survive the noose, hell, everything!'

As the flames rose higher, Angelica put a hand to her brow. A moment later the heat made her stumble forward.

Elmer sneered. Then, with a lightning reaction, he swung the gun back towards Jeff. Without much hope, Jeff jerked his gun up to aim at Elmer, but long before he reached him a shot pealed out.

Jeff still moved his arm up and, thinking he'd got lucky a second time, he picked out Elmer's heart. He fired, but Elmer was already falling backwards, a bloom spreading across his chest while his head jerked backwards.

Jeff's shot only made him flinch before he fell from view behind the spreading flames. Jeff hurried away from the scorching heat to Angelica's side where, to his surprise, he found that Deputy Bell was already helping her.

Bell had been crawling along behind her, Jeff now realized, while staying hidden from Elmer's view.

Bell took one arm and Jeff the other. They dragged Angelica to the doorway, where Jeff looked back. The fire was spreading rapidly and now it surrounded Elmer, who lay on his back amidst the flames, looking upward.

Then his hand twitched and he reached for the pocket where he kept the Bible that Angelica had given him.

Then the heat became too fierce and Jeff had to retreat with Bell and Angelica.

By the time they reached the main door, the roof was ablaze. Outside Verena and three other nuns were tending to the other patients they'd brought out from elsewhere in the hospital.

Jeff and Bell handed Angelica over to Verena's care, receiving only a grumbled demand from Angelica to stop manhandling her. Then, after getting assurance that all the patients were accounted for, they turned back to the hospital.

The firm-jawed look the two men shot at each other confirmed that they both reckoned they couldn't stop the fire from spreading now.

'Did Angelica know you were hiding behind her?' Jeff asked.

'It was her idea,' Bell said. He leaned towards him. 'But don't let on that I told you.'

Jeff smiled. 'Do you believe me now that Elmer was responsible for everything that happened?'

Bell tipped back his hat as he considered the burning hospital.

'I now think that more went on here than I was aware of.' He sighed. 'Perhaps you and I should have been fighting on the same side.'

Jeff nodded. Then he watched the flames. Only when the roof caved in did he finally accept that Elmer wouldn't be coming out. He leaned towards Bell.

'Where's Dewey?' he asked.

'He told me he'd cover my back in case Elmer got past me.' Bell looked around and frowned. 'I assume he's doing that somewhere.'

CHAPTER 16

'Maybe now,' Jeff said, considering the burnt-out wreckage of the hospital, 'you'll accept that you were wrong about Elmer Drake.'

He turned to face Sister Angelica's wide open and annoyed eyes.

'I won't accept that,' she declared. 'It's not for me to judge whether a man should be redeemed or not. All I do is help the sick and injured.'

Jeff conceded this point by craning his neck to look over the extent of the damage to the hospital. Overnight the ferocious heat had cooled so that now only the occasional flurry of smoke was rising up. The roof and everything within had been destroyed, but the stone walls had survived intact.

'I hope you'll be able to help the sick and injured again soon.'

'We will.' She removed the jewelled cross from her neck. 'I've avoided using this for a long time, but perhaps now is the time to sell it and use the money for a worthwhile cause.'

Jeff nodded. Several nuns were starting to work their way through the debris while Verena tended to the patients.

He watched her, hoping she'd look at him. When she didn't, he turned to Angelica.

'Is there anything I can do to help before I leave?'

'Getting out of our way is the most useful thing you can do.' Angelica considered the nuns and then lowered her voice. 'Although it would aid me if you were to say goodbye to Cynthia.'

'You mean Sister Verena.'

'I know what I said.'

Jeff considered Angelica's thin smile and then nodded. He walked over to Verena. He stood behind her and waited until she'd finished dealing with her patient's bandages, although her frequent fumbling showed that she knew he was there.

'I'm going now,' he said when she turned to him.

She bowed her head, but she didn't reply for so long that Jeff started to wonder if she would speak.

'I wish you good fortune,' she said at last in a small voice, 'no matter where your journey takes you.'

'And the same to you, even if your journey is a shorter one.'

This appeared to be the right thing to say as she looked up.

'It's one I may struggle with, as I knew I would.'

Jeff couldn't think what was the right thing to say to this, so he withdrew the damaged locket from his pocket.

'This is all that's left of Cynthia Harris. What should I do with it?'

She watched the locket turn in the sun until it came to rest. Then she held out a hand.

'I'll keep it.'

'I didn't think you were allowed to keep possessions from your old life.'

'I'm not.' She looked past him to consider Angelica. 'But one day soon I'll be ready to give it away again.'

Then, having spoken in a positive way about the turmoil that her recent experience with Elmer had caused her, she took the locket from him.

'As you wish,' Jeff said.

He backed away slowly, giving her enough time to speak but also the opportunity to be silent.

'We were both affected deeply by what happened to my family,' she said. 'I chose to help the sick and you chose to right injustices. We both became different people from the ones we might have become, but I reckon the changes were for the better.'

'I think so too,' Jeff said. 'Goodbye, Cynthia.'

'And goodbye to you, Jeff.' She considered for a moment and then opened the locket to look at the inside and the initials scratched there. 'And to the children we once were.'

She favoured him with an easy smile that made him think about what his life might have been like if Elmer had never visited Dirtwood. Unlike the nun, he reckoned it would have been a better life, but he

158

still returned the smile.

'In that case, goodbye, Sister Verena.' Jeff turned away.

Angelica was busying herself elsewhere and nobody else was looking his way. So he headed to his horse. At a gallop he rode away from the hospital, through the entrance to the gorge, and then on across the plains to Redemption.

He didn't look back.

When he arrived in town, he rode past the saloon where he'd met Dewey Shark and carried on to the law office. He dismounted and examined the Wanted posters outside, as he had done many times before in many different towns.

He found that overnight Deputy Bell had posted a new one. It was for Dewey Shark and this time there was a bounty on his head.

Jeff ignored it and picked another one.